MASQUERADE PARTY MURDER

JUNIPER HOLIDAY BOOK 4

LEIGHANN DOBBS

"Madam, the DJ wants to know where you would like her to set up her equipment in the ballroom."

Juniper, hip deep in feather boas of every color, looked over her shoulder in surprise at her ghost butler, Lionel. "She can see you?"

"No, madam. I overheard her talking to Terrence."

"Ah," Juniper said and went back to sorting through the mess of feathers. "Did he tell her where to set up? He already knows. I told him earlier today."

"I was not aware of this, mum," Lionel intoned.

"Well, I didn't tell you, Lionel, because you

can't exactly relay my instructions to anyone," Juniper remarked distractedly.

"Of course not, mum."

Juniper stopped flinging feathery strangle scarves around, her shoulders lifting and lowering quickly in a short sigh. That was Lionel's miffed tone. She'd said something to upset him. Dang it. "Lionel, I didn't mean—"

"It's quite all right, madam. You simply spoke the truth. I am dead. There is no denying the fact." He gave a slight bow, hands behind his back. "If you will excuse me, I must go see how Jacobi and Felicity are faring."

Instead of slowly sinking through the floor or floating across to the wall, Lionel vanished, and with his disappearance, Juniper leaned her head back and gave a great big sigh that she felt to her spinal cord. They were mere weeks out from Christmas, and she was feeling a bit weary. All this celebrating was her idea, yes, but lord, she could really use a rest.

And now she had a ghost with hurt feelings to deal with—on top of getting everything ready to go before tonight's big New Year's party. It was moments like this when she wished someone else could communicate with her ghostly staff.

Well… there *was* someone, but she'd rather not have to deal with old Quackers right now. She had to see him too much as it was. Of course, half of it wasn't her fault. It wasn't like she could keep people from falling dead or being found dead on her property. Desmond Mallard (or Quackers, as she sometimes referred to him) was a detective on the Crescent Cove police force, and he took his job seriously. Juni helped him out, though, on occasion. She figured it was the least she could do, considering how often he found himself out here when he clearly didn't want to be.

He didn't want her help, but she gave it anyway. It was her way of giving back. Whether he liked it or not.

"Sometimes you just can't win," Juniper said to the housecats, Ludo, Loki, and Finn. All three of them ignored her. Ludo was busy sniffing at the feathers, her dainty pink nose twitching. Loki had managed to get tangled in a fuchsia boa that looked striking against his black fur. Finn was too serious to play with feathers, so he lay atop the bed, watching the others with a detached air of slight disdain.

"June, you ready? Your guests are going to be here any minute," Juniper's goddaughter, Victoria, announced as she waltzed into Juniper's room without knocking.

Following closely behind was Barclay, her beloved Jack Russell-and-Chihuahua mix. Barclay's eyes lit up when he saw the cats playing with the boas, and he raced over. Ludo hissed and ran under the bed. Loki jumped up onto a bureau. Finn snuggled deeper into the pillows on the bed. Barclay simply looked around as if wondering why everyone had run away.

Shooting a glare over her shoulder at her goddaughter, Juniper said, hands spread out before her, "Does it look like I'm ready?"

Tori blinked, looking around at the stacks of clothes lying scattered about the room. "Whoa. You having trouble picking out an outfit? I thought you had already decided what you were going to wear."

"This is from days ago," Juniper said. "Well, most of it. And I did. It's on the bed. I'm trying to untangle this pile of feathery horrors I've collected over the years. There's a specific one I need, and I think it's in the middle of the knot."

"Give it here," Tori said, waving her hands.

Juniper tossed it over without hesitation and got to her feet. "Thanks, Tor. I've gotta go talk to Lion-o. I hurt his feelings earlier and need to apologize. Let me know when you're done!"

"Juniper Holiday, you are not about to leave me to sort this mess myself!"

"I'll be back!" Juniper said cheerily, giving Tori a big smile before she closed the door behind her.

Tori's irate voice followed her as she escaped down the stairs.

"Juniper!"

She power walked barefoot across the marble floors, ducking into one room after another in search of her long-dead butler, calling his name and getting no response.

Her search garnered more than a few looks from the decorators and serving staff as they went about their tasks setting up for the party, but Juniper ignored them. They knew the place was "rumored" to be haunted and that she had been caught talking to thin air more than once.

If they hadn't caught on by now that it wasn't an act, then whatever.

"Juniper Holiday, tell me I haven't missed my chance."

Skidding to a halt in the middle of the hall leading to one of the many living rooms, Juniper turned and stared in wide-eyed astonishment at her unannounced guest, not quite believing what she was seeing. Tall and dark-haired with a boyish face and a mischievous grin, Chalis McGregor stood with his shoulder propped against the wall.

Juniper smiled. Her old buddy hadn't changed a bit.

"Chalis McGregor. I don't believe it! What are you doing here? I thought you were living it up with a princess somewhere in the Swiss Alps."

Juniper knew that Chalis was trying to buy the old abandoned mansion down the road from her, but Mayor Berkshaw had been giving him a hard time, saying the property needed to be condemned and couldn't be sold. Chalis had big plans for it, a total renovation with swimming pools and tennis courts. He had the money for it too. Why the mayor would rather have the property continue to go to ruin instead of letting Chalis renovate it was a mystery. Maybe he just didn't want Chalis coming to town. The two did have somewhat of an adversarial history.

"June. Babe. I never said she was a princess, only that she was *my* princess," Chalis said, casually walking over to her. "And we broke up a few years ago. I've been flying solo ever since." He grinned and hugged her close, ending the embrace with a loud kiss on her cheek. "How ya been, sweetheart?"

"I'm great!" she answered, grinning back. "You're a little early for the party, though. How did you even get in?"

"Butler let me in. I figured I'd come early so we could catch up."

"That sounds great, except right now, I'm looking for my dead butler. Go make yourself at home in the front parlor, and I'll be back in a few." Juniper gestured toward the front parlor and walked away, leaving Chalis staring after her. As she continued her search for Lionel, she couldn't help but wonder why Chalis had resurfaced now after so many years being away. And if he was here, in Crescent Cove, did that mean *he* was somewhere nearby?

Her stomach flipped at the thought. Back in the day, Chalis, *he*, and Juniper had been the gilded trio. But that was before…. She shook her head, refusing to go down that rabbit hole right now. She had a party to get ready for and a butler to find. Now was not the time to get lost in broken-hearted memories.

CHAPTER TWO

$\mathcal{L}$ionel could not be found. He'd disappeared completely—a feat quite easy for a ghost—obviously not wanting to be located, even for an apology. Juniper had searched the house up and down several times, but nothing had come of it. Finally, there was no time. If she wanted this party to be all she had touted, she needed to dress and get downstairs.

"Tori, sweets, can you please run on down there and make sure the valet parking folks don't crowd my private garage? If something like what happened at Thanksgiving were to happen again, I'm really gonna need to be able to get the car out."

Tori was already dressed and ready for tonight's big gala. Her sequined red dress sparkled, even without the flash of strobes and multicolored party lights. She pulled the ivory handheld opera mask away from her eyes and nodded. "Sure. I'll hop down there right quick. You hurry up, June. This is your big New Year's celebration party, after all. You can't be late— not even for Lionel."

As Tori rushed away to see to the parking situation, Juniper huffed a sigh. She still wanted to get downstairs far enough ahead of the first guest so she could spend a few minutes catching up with Chalis.

"As if there's not enough otherwise to distract me," she grumbled while pulling her dress over her head. "The music's already started!"

She hummed in time with the tune and pulled on this and that until, at last, she was ready. Her long, flowing white silk gown streamed around her. The silver-trimmed mask she'd chosen for the evening slid easily over her face, its curling blue, silver, and white streamers spilling down from the sides almost to the floor. She hastily tucked her feet into a pair of white satin slippers and raced for the bedroom door and ran down the stairs.

"June. You look like a goddess, girl!" Chalis said. He must have gotten tired of sitting in the front parlor and was waiting for her at the bottom of the stairs. His eyes twinkled behind his mask, and he held out his hand. "Shall we?"

Juniper snorted. "Are you sure you still can, Chal? This song has quite a jumping vibe."

His expression one of wounded playfulness, Chalis MacGregor took three steps back and broke into dance.

Juniper laughed. "All right, all right. You've still got it. Now, get me out there on the floor so I can get it too!"

It wasn't long before guests started streaming in, and Juniper left Chalis with a young woman in a fuchsia chiffon minidress and long blond hair.

Soon, the mansion was filled with masked guests in their finest gowns and tuxedos. It was a sea of sequins, silks, and velvets. With everyone wearing masks, it was a little difficult to recognize who was who, but Juniper greeted everyone as if they were her best friend while waitstaff circled the room with trays of drinks and hors d'oeuvres.

For the next two hours, Juniper made her rounds, chatting with everyone she could possibly bump into—and with the music she had chosen and the way she danced, she bumped into quite a lot of people. Besides Chalis, who she adored and spent a great deal of time with, she'd also spent a moment chatting with Preston Lane. The man who was currently wed to one of those flashy movie starlets was standing alone. She couldn't help but notice there was more of the cold steel in his eyes she knew showed up when he was dealing with something, but with so many people here at the mansion tonight, there was no appropriate time to pull him aside to ask what was going on.

William Walcroft, one of the Cove's most prominent bankers, was also in attendance. He'd come with his wife, Donna. William, though he'd made time to converse, seemed to have another pressing agenda. He kept scanning the crowd—looking for the mayor, his wife told her in an aside. "He's probably hoping to have another go at him about that project he so wants to fund, but he said Mayor Berkshaw keeps asking for changes."

"What project is that?" Juniper asked, mostly to be polite.

Donna frowned. "I'm not sure. He's pretty secretive about it, but that's why he's had to visit the mayor's house a few times. I guess it's hush-hush."

"Aren't most of them?" Juniper joked and pushed another glass of champagne on Donna, who was getting a little clingy.

Fedora Layhee, Juniper's neighbor and friend, was there, of course. The RarelyDone Steakhouse werewolves too. Quincy from WitchRoast Cafe had declined, the same as Detective Mallard, though Juniper had extended an invite to him. Desmond had just flat out said no. Not that Juniper minded; quite the opposite. She was just as delighted to have him *not* be in attendance tonight.

All in all, despite her lingering worry over the upset between her and Lionel, Juniper decided her party was a smashing success. But it was now ten minutes to midnight. There was more excitement to come. The countdown, of course, would be exciting because that was when everyone would unmask. But there was also the spectacular fireworks show she'd planned. It was time to get everyone outside.

Juniper held up her hand in a signal to the DJ to stop the music and make the announcement, then she went ahead to the central set of double glass doors leading onto the back lawn and made her way out into the night, beneath a lovely covering of stars.

She'd had a stage of sorts set up in the center with a big countdown clock on it. That was where she would be when the fireworks started. She'd invited Tori, Fedora, and Chalis to join her.

The music had started up again, this time blaring from the speakers on the balcony railing, spilling through the chilly December air as the ushers she'd hired routed her partygoers out of the ballroom and into the night for the big countdown. Everyone had enough champagne in them that the cold winter air wasn't too much of a problem, though some of the men draped their jackets around their wives' shoulders.

When there were only three minutes to go, waiters and waitresses hurried through the crowd, handing out fresh glasses of champagne.

Tori, Fedora, Chalis, and Juniper were the last to receive theirs, and then the music shut off.

"Sixty seconds to midnight—are y'all ready?" Juniper called into the microphone. "At midnight exactly, the masks come off! Get set, everyone! From ten, let's count them down!"

The speaker cut, and all eyes were trained on the big countdown clock. Then, the crowd chanted in unison with Juniper: "Ten! Nine! Eight! Seven! Six!"

Juniper glanced around, noting as many masked faces as she could while making her guess as to who was lurking behind them.

"Five! Four! Three! Two! One!"

A superloud horn sounded at the exact stroke of twelve. A storm of beribboned masks filled the air just as the first of the fireworks went off and exploded into the sky above them. Tori gasped, looking into the crowd instead of the colorful display of lights in the sky. "June! Isn't that Mayor Berkshaw?"

Juniper glanced in the direction she'd indicated to see the mayor stumbling around. A tall woman, still masked, stood at his side.

"Is he drunk? Who is that with him?" His wife, Susan, had told Juniper she'd be out of town and wasn't flying in until shortly before midnight and probably wouldn't be able to make it. She'd sent her regrets, saying she hoped the party was a smashing success. As if it wouldn't be. All of Juniper's parties were successful—even if, lately, they turned into crime scenes.

As Juniper watched, the woman lowered her mask. "It's Madison Lane! I was wondering if she was here. But why is she with the mayor and not Preston?"

Tori clutched Juniper's arm. "Never mind that, Juniper. I think he's been shot!"

Juniper's brows snapped together. "Shot? Who has? Tor, what in the world are you talking about? That loud bang was the fireworks." Juniper gestured toward the sky as more fireworks went off above them.

"We have to hurry!" she told Juniper. Tori grabbed her godmother's hand and raced into the crowd. Then, just as suddenly, she ground to a halt. Mayor Berkshaw lay on the ground, his pristine white shirt now gone crimson. Madison Lane was kneeling in the snow beside him.

Berkshaw had been shot? Juniper's gaze immediately scanned the crowd, looking for the shooter.

People were milling about, many not even realizing someone had been shot. The fireworks were still going on, drawing everyone's attention. Only a few of the people nearby were slowly starting to realize what had happened. She didn't see anyone running away. Could someone have shot the mayor and then turned around and pretended to watch the fireworks?

There was one person Juniper didn't see: her old friend Chalis. Was it any coincidence that Chalis suddenly appeared in town the very night Mayor Berkshaw was shot?

CHAPTER THREE

*J*uniper's mind was racing. She needed to do damage control… even though the damage was kind of already done, and everyone was currently gawking at it. And *everyone* was talking. Whispering. Staring. Pointing.

"June, we need to get everyone out of here," Tori said next to her in a quiet voice. "If they get too close—oh my God, no! No, absolutely not! Put the phone away, Gina! Don't you look at me like that. This poor man is dead. The least you can do is leave the cameras out of it."

Gina Dodd was from the local news station and always ready to be the first with a scoop.

Tori looked at Juniper imploringly. "Juni! Hurry up!"

Snapping out of her daze, Juniper snapped her fingers. "Right."

Lifting the mic that she still held in her hand, she spoke into it, her voice projected through the speakers. "Okay, folks. Let's move inside, move along. There we go. Yep, just head on back into the ballroom. Terrence, if you can hear me, close the drapes when everyone's inside, please. Thank you."

Slowly, the crowd dispersed, leaving only Juniper, Tori, and the dead mayor. Juniper watched as the heavy royal-blue drapes fell across the windows, and only then did she let herself breathe easier. She looked at Tori, hands on her hips. "Why the crud buckets does this crap keep happening to me?"

"Juni, I hardly think now is the time to make it about you," Tori remarked. "I better call the police."

A bone-chilling scream rent the air. "Floyd! No!" Susan Berkshaw came running from the side of the house. Apparently, she'd made it after all, but she wasn't dressed for the party. She had on slacks and a blouse under her fur coat. She threw herself on the snow next to the body.

"I heard about the shooting in the taxi on the way home from the airport." She blubbered as big fat tears streaked down her face.

Gina had worked fast getting the news out, apparently.

Tori knelt beside Susan, careful to keep her shoes and dress from the dark stain spreading across the snow.

"Mrs. Berkshaw," she said, her tone soft and kind, "I know this is a difficult time, but we should probably go inside. You don't have to stay with the others, but we need to keep the scene from getting contaminated."

Susan sniffled. Her makeup was ruined, black streaks running down her cheeks and dripping onto her chest and the ground. She shook her head. "I don't care. I don't want to leave him."

"I know," Tori said gently. "I know, but the police will be here soon, with an ambulance. We should at least be calm when they get here, okay? They're probably going to ask questions, and we need to be able to answer them clearly, yeah?"

Susan looked at her, clarity slowly coming to her eyes, and she sniffled some more before nodding. "Y-yeah. Okay. Yes, you're right. I do need to—yes. Okay."

Tori helped the woman stand and walked her back to the estate, giving Juniper a quick look before she left.

Detective Ackers arrived first, and Juniper left him with the body, eager to get inside before Mallard showed up.

She took another route that wouldn't put her in contact with her guests just yet, shaking her head and talking to herself the whole way. She needed a moment alone to think before she tried to address the masses. Catching Terrence before she disappeared, she told him where she was going and to only come get her if things really started getting out of control.

"Oh, and tell 'em not to leave, Terry. If I know Quackman, he's going to want to talk to everybody, and I mean *everybody*. So. They're gonna be here a while. I'll be in to keep 'em entertained in a few, but right now, I need a minute. If you have to, find Tori and tell her to keep an eye on things until I get there. Okay?"

"Yes, ma'am."

"Cool beans."

That taken care of, Juniper practically ran to the library, her heels clacking on the marble floor the whole way. But no sooner had she entered the library and taken a much-needed breath than the door opened behind her, smacking her in the back and nearly making her go sprawling across the floor.

"Aaack!"

"Oops! I'm so sorry, June. I thought you were trying to escape, and I wanted to catch you before you did."

Juniper leveled a seething glare at her friend. "What the actual heck, Fedora?"

Fedora gave her an apologetic look. "I said I was sorry."

Juniper waved her hand. "What do you need?"

"Well… I thought maybe you could use an ear? You know, to bounce your theories and ideas off of since Victoria is occupied with the mayor's wife. I know you usually discuss things with her, but since she's not here…"

"You want to be the Watson to my Holmes."

Fedora grinned. "Yes."

"All right, sit down," Juniper told her. She

wasn't too miffed, since she had come in here to try and get things worked out in her head anyway. Having Fedora here to listen would probably help. She wasn't Tori, but she was better than empty air. She probably only had a few minutes before the ghosts showed up, anyway, throwing their ideas about what happened at her. Hopefully, Lionel had forgiven her.

Settling on the settee, she looked at Fedora. "There's at least three people I think could've done it," she said. "Preston Lane, Chalis McGregor, and William Walcroft. They all had motive. They all had opportunity. All we gotta do is connect the dots and *bam*! We'll have our killer."

Fedora scrunched up her face. "Wait… how does Preston have motive?"

"He seemed troubled, and I heard he was having problems with a project. Something about the mayor shutting him down."

Fedora looked skeptical. "I saw Madison arguing with the mayor. And what were the two of them whispering about at the edge of the crowd when he was shot?"

"Good question. Come to think of it, she disappeared pretty quickly after that."

Fedora's brows shot up. "You don't think she was the one that shot him, do you?"

Juniper frowned. "I don't know. I guess we'll have to find out how far away the shooter was. Why would she, though?"

Fedora shrugged. "People have all kinds of motives. Maybe he spurned her advances."

Juniper laughed. "Seriously? She's married to Preston Lane. Why would she make advances to the mayor?"

Fedora leaned forward, a knowing look in her eye. "Power. The mayor has power, and maybe Madison wanted some of it. I heard someone at the mayor's mansion was having a torrid affair."

"Who told you that?"

Fedora pressed her lips together. "I can't say. But it was someone reliable."

"Maybe." Juniper was doubtful about beautiful Madison Lane and stodgy old Mayor Berkshaw having an affair but didn't want to rule anyone out.

"And Chalis and William? What is their motive?" Fedora asked.

Juniper grimaced. "I hate to even say anything about Chalis, but he's been trying to buy and renovate the old Marston mansion, and Mayor Berkshaw was putting up roadblocks. Said the place should be condemned and turned into a park. And William was very busy scanning the crowd. He seemed distracted, and his wife told me that he's been trying to get funding for a project and the mayor hasn't been receptive."

"Juniper! Those hardly seem like motives to kill. I bet there are tons of people that have better reasons. Like his wife, for example. It's usually the spouse anyway."

"True, but I don't think that is the case here. Susan Berkshaw wasn't even here when he was shot. She'd been driving back from the airport."

"Hmm." Fedora chewed a nail as she thought. "One thing we know for sure is that someone here has a gun. Hopefully, the police will find it on them, and then we'll know who the killer is."

"Maybe they don't have it on them anymore. That would be dumb. And besides, no one had their coats on since we'd all come out from the ballroom. Where would they hide it on their person in those skimpy gowns and tight tuxes? I would think someone would notice a gun bulge pretty easily."

"Good point. They probably hid it in the house. Which means the police will have to search it."

Juniper pressed her lips together. "That's a lot of house to search. Hopefully, that doesn't mean that Detective McDuck will be here for days on end. If I have to ramp up the sleuthing to figure out who the killer is to get rid of him, then so be it."

After meeting with Fedora, Juniper figured she'd better check in on Susan Berkshaw and give Tori a break. Tori had brought Susan to one of the smaller sitting rooms so that she wouldn't have to deal with the crowd in her devastated state, and Juni felt it was her duty to sit with her until the police were ready to interview the widow. Tori slipped out of the room after Juni entered.

Susan was standing at the window, looking outside. She turned, revealing that her eyes were red and mascara tracks still ran down her cheeks. Juni noticed a dusting of blood on her white fur coat.

"Maybe you should sit. Can I get you something to calm your nerves? Brandy maybe?"

Susan looked at the gold silk brocade couch where Juniper was indicating for her to sit as if she were having a hard time processing the words. "Yes. I suppose. Maybe a brandy would be good." She slowly made her way to the couch and sat.

Juniper poured brandy from a crystal decanter into a tumbler and brought it to Susan. "Can I take your coat?"

"Oh, no thanks. I feel chilled." Susan shivered.

Juniper sat next to her. "I'm so sorry about your husband."

Maybe she shouldn't have said that, because it set off a barrage of tears. Juniper held out a box of tissues.

Susan grabbed a wad of them and blew her nose and dabbed at her eyes. "Thank you. It's just so sudden. Doesn't seem real yet. I just can't believe it. Who would do such a thing?"

"That's a good question. Do you know anyone who would want to kill him?"

"Floyd? No! Well, maybe… he did have control of a lot of things, being mayor and all, and not everyone agreed with him."

Juniper thought about how he was holding up Chalis's house plans… who else's future was he messing with?

"Was there anyone in particular that was mad at him?" Juniper asked.

Susan shook her head. "Not that I can think of. He always managed to smooth things over. He could be quite charming when he wanted to. At least the ladies seemed to think so."

Susan's voice shook at that last part.

"The ladies? You don't think that he…" Juniper let her voice trail off. She didn't want to make Susan feel worse, but it would be valuable information if Susan thought her husband was fooling around. And besides, she'd opened the door with that last comment.

Susan sighed. "I have a few suspicions, but now that he's gone, it hardly seems to matter."

"It might matter since he was murdered," Juniper blurted out.

Susan started blubbering again and grabbed more tissues.

Ackers poked his head into the room. "Detective Mallard is ready to talk to you now, Mrs. Berkshaw."

Susan sniffled and nodded. "I'm ready."

Juniper patted Susan's hand. "Let me know if you need anything," she said before hurrying out of the room.

CHAPTER FOUR

CVN-21 TV News, Crescent Cove General, Crescent Cove Fire Department, at least three different paparazzi vans, *Cove Daily* newspaper, and half the city council (the half that weren't already invited to her New Year's Eve masked ball, that is) were hanging around her front lawn.

Juniper was losing track of how many different groups had shown up at her place since the clock had struck midnight and the fireworks went off. She dropped the heavy drapes back into place and turned away from the window—blocking out the reminder of what her wonderful celebration to ring in a bright and brilliant new year had devolved into in barely an hour.

Once word went out that the mayor was the one who got shot, cars and sirens and people came in like Noah's flood. Juniper had retreated to a back parlor with Tori for a few seconds of peace.

"How is Susan Berkshaw?" Tori asked.

"Shaken. I left her in the library with a glass of brandy and Detective Mallard. She happened to mention that she suspected the mayor of having an affair, maybe more than one, even."

"Juniper! Please tell me you didn't interrogate her." Tori gave her a reproachful look.

"I didn't. She just sort of blurted it out. But Fedora had heard rumors about an affair too."

"Huh, well, that gives Susan motive, doesn't it? Why would she blurt out something that would give her a motive for murder?" Tori asked.

Juniper mulled that over for a few seconds. "I guess she knows she'd be proven innocent since she wasn't at the party. She said she was driving home from the airport and heard it on the radio, so that gives her an alibi."

Tori nodded. "I guess so. That means it must have been one of the partygoers."

Juniper sighed at the thought of the partygoers, the police, and the news crews trampling about. "My house is going to be a wreck after this."

Tori's wry smile was accompanied by a gentle pat on Juniper's shoulder. "The house is always a wreck after one of your parties, Juni. We'll get it back in order, just like last time and the time before that. Everything will be ship-shape again before we have to think about Valentine's Day."

"If there *is* a Valentine's Day celebration, Tori. Have you been listening to what they're saying?" Juniper walked over to the sofa and sat, folding her legs underneath her as she did so, then she lay back against both the back and arm of the thing. If she weren't careful, she could just cuddle up and take a nap.

As if sensing she needed comfort, Ludo jumped up on the sofa and snuggled next to her. Not to be outdone in the attention department, Finn settled on her other side. Loki rested down by Juniper's feet.

"I heard someone say this place is turning

out to be a hotbed for murder, not to mention the scandal I create just by being me on the daily. One lady wondered if I am setting these things up for entertainment! Can you believe that? As if I have to resort to such despicable horror to make my parties worth attending. Believe you me, I'd much rather never have to deal with murder."

"They're just curious, suspicious, and in the dark, June. They feel confused, so they're taking potshots at you. Ignore them." She sat in a chair and shrugged. "The person you really need to worry about isn't even here. Yet."

"Mr. McQuack-a-doodle? He actually is here," she said, her face squished up to indicate what she thought about the detective's presence. "Sabrina let him in through the kitchen about ten minutes ago. I think she even made sure he had a snack before he turned himself loose on the two hundred and fifty or so possible murderers in our ballroom."

Juniper didn't miss the little flicker of something in Tori's eye, but like her goddaughter, she pretended not to notice. "Look, Tori, I think we have other things to worry about than the detective you're starting to be sweet on. Like Chalis.

And us. I mean, this is the fourth time Duckbutt and his waddlers have had to show up at one of my celebrations... twice because of a murder that actually occurred right here at the house!"

Tori rubbed at her temples and nodded her agreement. "I get what you're saying, June. This is starting to mar your personal reputation, right? I could see how pained you were about it when you mentioned that lady talking about how you might be setting the stage for these things and all."

"It's over half the town, Tor." Juniper groaned. "Over. Half. The. Town! How do I fix something like this? See, my boat or bag or whatever you wanna call it, is spreading happiness and laughter, fun, joy, cheer. How could anybody in the Cove think I'd have some malicious part in all this doom and gloom and destruction of lives?"

"They just don't know you, Juniper. That's all. If they knew you like me and Chalis and Fedora, why, they'd love you as much as we do. Not one person would ever dare whisper such lies against you." Tori slid off her stilettos and rubbed at her feet with both hands. "Ugh. The next time we have a little get-together like this, remind me heels are for sitting. My feet feel like they're about to fall off!"

"Maybe I should just stop, you know? No more celebrations. No more parties. No more trying to put a few bright spots into the middle of people's mostly mediocre lives."

Tori was shaking her head no before Juniper even finished. "We can't. *You* can't."

"Why can I not? Believe me, I definitely can if things like this don't stop happening on my watch, sweetie."

"You won't stop, June. I know this because I know you. This stuff is what you love. Celebrating life is... well, it's a part of who you are. You're not going to stop, because despite what has happened these past few months, the people of the Cove love it too. They love your parties. They love the invites—makes them feel noticed. Counted. Special, you know? And they love the dressing up. The food. The music."

Slightly mollified, Juniper said, "For how long, though? I mean, eventually, someone is going to make a big, fat, hairy public deal out of the bit about bad things happening where I am, and the proverbial spit is gonna splatter through the also proverbial fan. What then?"

Tori sighed and slipped her shoes back on before standing to offer her godmother a hand up. "I expect you'll be all over it when and if that time ever comes, Juni dearest, but for now…"

"I know, I know," Juniper said as she let Tori help her off the couch. "I can't hide in here forever."

Tori nodded. "Exactly."

CHAPTER FIVE

As soon as Juniper entered the ballroom, lyrics from Golden Earring's "Twilight Zone" played in her head. The place was very much a madhouse. There was even a gun... somewhere. Somebody had the murder weapon. Juniper just hoped they hadn't tried to stash it somewhere on her property. She didn't need anyone's bad mojo stinking up the place.

Speaking of bad mojo, she probably should talk to Quincy about doing a sage sweep just to make sure nothing was lingering after the last few months.

The sound of hundreds of people talking at once, even hushed as their voices were, was like static white noise in Juniper's ears. Like clockwork, one person noticed her, and the rest followed, turning the calm gathering into a seething mass.

"Juniper!"

"What happened?"

"Did you see who did it?"

"Who shot the mayor, June?"

"Did you see it happen?"

"Was it gross?"

She held her hands up in front of her. "Whoa, whoa, whoa. One thing at a time, please. I don't know why y'all are asking me these things. I wasn't with him when it happened. I was privy to the information about the same time all of you were, which was after the fact. It appears that he was shot. I have no idea who did it, and yeah, it was gross."

Voices rose as her guests clamored for more, pressing closer to ask their questions at the same time instead of one at a time, or not at all, which was what she would have preferred. She didn't see a single reporter in the mix, so why they were all trying to get answers from her was a bit annoying.

"I'm going to need everybody to calm down, please," a vaguely familiar voice commanded. It took her a second to recall from where exactly, and when she did, her eyes went wide, and she ducked down behind Tori, peeking over the top of her shoulder.

"Hide me before the Duck-Man cometh!"

She could almost feel Tori roll her eyes. "Would you stop? Desmond isn't even in the room."

"How do you know?" Juniper hissed, her eyes scanning the crowd. "There's a bazillion people in here."

"There's only something like three hundred, June."

"Yeah, well, that's not nearly enough to keep him from finding me."

Tori glanced over her shoulder at June. "Why are you worried about running into the detective? You two should be bosom buddies by now."

Juniper's mouth dropped open in shock. Then she glared at the back of Tori's head. "Bite your tongue, Victoria Evangeline Cooper."

"Only if you bite yours first."

Juniper scoffed. "You wish."

Tori didn't respond for a second, then she

said, "Okay, I think you can stand back up now and stop using me as your personal shield. David has them more or less corralled."

"Who's David?"

"Detective Haverman. His first name is David. Detective Ackers's name is Sean, and Detective Nichols's is Harvey."

"You spend too much time with the enemy, girl."

Tori clicked her tongue. "They are not our enemies, June."

Juniper flapped her hand back and forth in front of her, her eyes rolling. "I know they're not *really*, but it's fun to pretend. Plus it gets a rise out of Duckie-Doo, and that makes my day immediately brighter."

Tori side-eyed her. "You've got to get a different hobby, June."

"I could always bug you instead."

"Let's not."

"Then the Duckster it is."

"You're going to give that poor man health problems, stressing over your antics all the time."

Juniper snorted. "His job is going to stress him out before I do. Besides, I think he secretly likes butting heads with me. Keeps him on his toes."

"Keeping this crowd calm and in one place should keep you on yours," Tori said. "They're starting to get restless again."

Juniper heaved a put-upon sigh. "Fine. I'll calm the masses. Watch me and see how it's done, Tor. You'll need to know these things when I've moved on."

"You're going to be running things from beyond the grave, Juniper."

"Then you best be figuring out how to communicate with the ghosts here, dear, because I'm not about to jump through hoops to tell you how to settle a crowd," Juniper said as she walked away.

She moved from group to group because people always seemed to move in herds, like with like and all that, calming them down, asking about their families, explaining things to the best of her ability until she might as well have recorded it on tape and played it on repeat through the stereo system.

She perked up at the idea for a second but then thought better of it because if there was one thing she didn't want to hear on repeat, it was herself talking. And every song she thought she could play was probably inappropriate for the moment because, of course, her dark sense of humor would be wreaking havoc with her music choices right now. The first one that came to mind was Queen's "Another One Bites the Dust." She didn't think anyone would appreciate that, especially not the grieving widow.

"Juniper Holiday, are we going to be here all night?"

Turning to address the speaker, one Cora Liann Phelps of the Historical Society—an elderly lady with strict features, a rigid stature, but the twinkle of remembered misspent youth in her eyes—Juniper said, "It depends on how long it takes them to ferret out the killer, and there's a lot of people to go through."

Cora's eyes widened marginally. "So it is one of us?"

Juniper's eyes narrowed. "Indeed, it must be." She leaned close and widened her eyes theatrically. "The killer is in this very room!"

By the time Detective Mallard and his duckaroos cleared the mansion, it was well after four a.m., and Juniper was feeling literally beaten. Not that she had been—God forbid they add assault to what had happened here tonight!—but she sure felt like it. "Ugh! I just want to crawl in bed and sleep until the middle of January."

Tori's snort said she knew what was coming. Whine. "Why so specific about when you'd like to wake?"

Juniper sat up from where she'd leaned over on one of the tables they'd set up in the ball-room, a bit of a glimmer of excitement peeking through the exhaustion in her eyes. "Because I'll need time to prepare for the Valentine's Day Exchange and Raffle, you know. I can't just pull these megaparties out of a hat. Such perfect execution takes planning."

"Yeesh." Tori's cringe might have been comical to witness if Juniper weren't so tired. "Maybe 'execution' was not the best word, considering."

"Right."

Tori pushed back in her chair and sighed. "So what do we do until mid-January, June?"

"That was funny, Tor." Her shoulders shook from the chuckle she tried to suppress. "January June."

Her chuckle turned to sputtering laughter. The sound of it made Tori smile. After a minute, she was howling with laughter, just like Juniper.

"What in the world has gotten into you two ladies?" Desmond Mallard asked, making them both jump at the unexpected other voice in the room. "Do you not realize the severity of what happened here tonight?"

Juniper stood and tugged her dress into a more appropriate shape. "Of course we realize. Doesn't mean humor is no longer allowed, does it? I mean, there were two months in a row, back-to-back, and it was funny—especially as they were very out of order."

Tori bit back another giggle then said, "It's late, Detective. We are all a bit punchy. I think June may even be night high, so why don't you say what you've come to say and leave so we can all get to bed? Tonight has been exhausting."

Desmond looked confused. "Night high?"

Waving away his concern, Tori said, "That time when you're too sleepy to know exactly what you're doing or why you're doing it, and everything that gets said or done is hilarious. You know, night high."

When her explanation made no dent in his confusion, she pushed the champagne glasses to one side and motioned for him to sit. "Before you decide you need to order up a blood test, why don't you sit here and give us your list of demands so you can go home. You look tired, Detective."

Beside her, Juniper almost choked on stifled laughter. Tori's lips quirked, and she arched a brow. "How's that for managing an awkward moment, Junie baby?"

"Hilarious," Juniper told her. "You'll probably even regret it when you think back on it in the morning, so I'll tell you what—you run on upstairs and go nighty night, and I'll deal with the detective. This time."

Her mock shudder almost sent Tori off in gales again. Almost. She managed to contain her laughter somehow. To Juniper's surprise, she took the suggestion far more willingly than her godmother had expected she would. After a quick hug and a hurried "g'night," Tori left the ballroom without a backward glance, leaving Juniper to square off with the Duck Man by herself.

"So I take it that it wasn't as easy as finding a smoking gun on one of the guests?" Juniper asked.

"Afraid not."

"And you searched everyone?"

"Everyone and everywhere. Now, is there any way I can easily convince you to keep your nose out of this one, Ms. Holiday? If not, I can bring Ackers in to Mirandize you and lock you up until we discover the mayor's killer."

Juniper's brow rose sharply as she tried to decide if he'd issued a warning or a threat.

"On what charges, Mister? I don't think so,

and no to the other too. Did you not hear the whispers in that crowd tonight, Desmond Mallard?" She shook her head. "The Covians are starting to think I'm jinxed or cursed or that there are spirits attached to the mansion."

"There are," he reminded her, his voice deadpan, and she waved the facts away.

"Not the malevolent kind. My ghosts are the kindest, most helpful, gentlehearted—"

"Spirits," he interrupted. "Ms. Holiday, I've seen them myself. You definitely have spirits in this house. Are they instigating the darkness in the mansion of late?"

He peered at her, suspicion in his eyes, and despite her tiredness after the harrowing events of the night, Juniper felt her annoyance with him begin to rise. Still, for Tori's sake, she tried to placate him. "You just do your job, Duckie-Doo, and leave me alone to do mine."

If the look on his face over her comment had had a sound, it would have been a long, drawn-out groan of frustration and despair. "Yours? I would think a woman of your financial means would enjoy a nice long visit in the Bahamas—or the Bermuda Triangle, maybe—but as far as this investigation goes, you need to stay out of it, Juniper. The mayor being the victim makes this a very high-profile case, and it could get dangerous. Stay out of it, as you should do. The work to be done to find Mayor Berkshaw's killer is mine."

Juniper planted both feet solidly on the ballroom floor and stared at him without blinking. "And the work to be done to quiet these rumors about me and the mansion, which just happened to coincide with the mayor's murder, Mr. Mallard-naise, is mine. Now, go find your duck squad members and rout them outta here too. I've had enough of this evening and of you. I do believe it's time for you to fly."

Juniper pointed toward the ballroom exit, the chorus of REO Speedwagon's "Time for Me to Fly" playing in her head with every step he made in that direction.

CHAPTER SEVEN

It was supposed to be easy. List of names, list of reasons, narrow it down, knock it out until the one responsible was left.

It was never that easy. Not in real life. And, apparently, not in Juniper's life, either.

She was currently on the phone with Prunella Preenly, co-owner of the Dusty Buns Bakery in town. She'd called to order a baker's dozen of Sprinky Dinks 'cause she was kind of addicted to them now, and they'd ended up chatting for... well, over an hour now, and not about donuts.

The mayor's death was the most-talked-about topic of conversation in the Cove at the moment, and the fae folk were just as curious about who offed him as everyone else. Juniper had spent at least half an hour explaining everything that happened last night to Pru because she hadn't been there, and now they were pretty much shooting the breeze about Juniper's approach to the whole thing while Juniper munched on chips and dip left over from the party.

Even the paranormal citizens of the Cove knew she wasn't going to leave it alone.

"I don't know what I'm going to do, Nella. I've got too many people to choose from, and every one of them have motive, and there was plenty of opportunity. A crowd of people outside, no one paying attention to anybody else —and they were wearing masks, so there's another thing! Anonymity, right there! I know!"

She moved the dip away from Loki, who was sniffing at it, and reached for a chip only to hit nothing but crumbs. "Shoot. Nella, I've gotta go. My snackage just ran out, and I can't think on an empty stomach. All right, bye, babe."

She ended the call and got up from her desk, which was strewn with scribbled-on papers and various dishes she'd smuggled in from the kitchen to indulge in food and drink while she tried to make heads or tails of her list of suspects and their motives for killing their dearly departed mayor.

Opening the door to her office, she was immediately waylaid by her three ghostly staff members, each with varying expressions of excitement on their gray, gossamer-looking faces. She felt a pang of guilt at seeing Lionel. She still hadn't apologized to him properly, and she noticed he wouldn't look her in the eye. She was going to have to remedy that but not in front of the other two.

Her brows rose. "Is the apocalypse happening?"

Three nearly identical looks of confusion were shared between them before they looked back at her and shook their heads in unison.

"Not that we are aware of, mum," Lionel intoned, his deep, ghostly voice a hint less friendly than usual.

Juniper wiggled her pointer finger back and forth between the three of them. "What gives? The three of you waiting for me at the same time must mean something monumental has happened."

"Oh, it has, ma'am," Felicity said, her voice musical with her excitement. "We were hoping to discuss it with you in your office."

Juniper looked at each of them in turn, wondering what kind of information they had gotten their ghostly hands on. "All right, but give me a sec, okay? I've got to go raid the pantry for food. I ran out of chips, and I need brain fuel."

"We will await your return in your office, madam," Lionel informed her, and one by one, the three of them floated inside, Jacobi taking care not to go through her because it was an unpleasant feeling for both her and him.

A glance behind her showed them standing in a line in front of her desk with the three cats in front of them. Juniper shrugged. "I guess we're doing that, then."

Shaking her head at them, she made her way to the kitchen and grabbed enough snacks to feed a small army, evaded a scolding from Sabrina about spoiling lunch, then headed back to her office, where the ghostly trio still waited.

Laying out the goods on her desk, she popped open a bag of chips, cracked a can of soda, and took a drink, grimacing at the sweet burn down her throat, then burped like a demon was trying to speak through her. Clasping her hands together atop her desk, she said, "Okay. I'm all ears. Tell me the good stuff, peeps."

And that was when the overload began. Each of them had different sources, different stories, different leads, and when it all came together, it was a big old tangled mess.

"So let me get this straight." Juniper looked over her notes. "You searched everywhere and couldn't find the gun."

"That's correct," Lionel said. At least his expression was a little friendlier now. "And we didn't see the police take it, either."

Juniper leaned back in her chair. "If the police found it on someone, they would have arrested them, and no one has been arrested, as far as I know. That means the gun might still be here."

"Ahem." Jacobi made a ghostly coughing noise.

Juniper looked over at him. "Yes?"

"Well, it's just that, as you know, my sense of smell is quite keen—that's how I can tell that Sabrina is ruining most of the dishes. Too many spices, not enough lemon." Jacobi sniffed.

"And…" Juniper motioned with her hand for him to continue.

"Well, I did smell a sulfurous scent similar to gunpowder over by the ice bucket last night. I looked in, but all I saw was the fake ice. The gun could have been below that, but, being a ghost, I couldn't move the fake cubes to see."

"Which ice bucket?" Juniper had had dozens of them out with champagne cooling in each one.

"The giant one. On the side of the house."

"Ahh. The decoration." The grounds had been decorated with all kinds of oversized party items. Giant party hats, champagne glasses, and one giant ice bucket. It would make a good hiding place for a gun. But surely Mallard had looked there? Couldn't hurt to double-check, though.

"Did any of you happen to see the mayor doing anything odd?" Juniper asked.

"I saw him arguing with that actress, Madison Lane," Felicity said. "Her gown was lovely."

"Speaking of gowns, I did see a woman in a silver gown skulking around the edges of the party and ducking behind plants," Jacobi said.

Juniper made a face, trying to picture the party. She'd been busy circulating and talking to guests, but she vaguely recalled seeing someone who seemed to be somewhat of a wallflower. "Did you notice her, Lissy?"

"Sorry. I was busy watching the dance floor." Lissy swirled from side to side. "Oh, how I would love to dance again."

"Lionel?" Juniper asked.

Lionel glanced up at the ceiling. "I was not in attendance, as I didn't think my ghostly services were of any value."

Okay, apparently, he was still mad. Juniper tried to make nice. "Oh, Lionel, that's not true. You're very valuable."

Lionel harrumphed but seemed slightly mollified.

"One last thing."

"Yes?" the three of them said in unison.

"Did any of you notice Chalis McGregor after the shooting?"

Felicity scrunched up her face. "He was on the dance floor with that young blonde all night. But I'm not sure if I saw either of them after."

"I might have seen him near the bar," Jacobi said.

"Once Lissy and Jacobi summoned me, I was more interested in scouring the grounds for clues," Lionel said.

Juniper sighed. "Okay. Thanks, guys. You've been really helpful."

"Of course, madam," Lionel said, giving a little bow before leaving through the ceiling. At least he hadn't just disappeared like before. She was making progress. Jacobi nodded and floated through the door, while Lissy gave a curtsy and went through the west wall.

Juniper reached for her phone and called Tori. "Hon, come quick. The ghosts gave me some clues, and I want you to help me check one of them out."

She ignored Tori's mumbled "Probably" and ended the call then tossed the phone onto her desk and awaited her goddaughter's arrival. She frowned as a thought occurred to her, and she reached for her phone again. "I should tell her to stop by the kitchen and get ice cream."

Ten minutes later, Tori showed up with two bowls of chocolate ice cream. Juniper reached for one, but Tori pulled it away. "I'll let you have it if you promise to help me brainstorm some plot twists."

"Of course, Tori-bori. You know I love doing that." Juniper grabbed the bowl and scooped up a big spoonful.

"So what do you need help with?" Tori asked.

"The ghosts gave me some clues, and I was thinking you could help me check one out."

Tori's brow shot up. She spooned another glob of ice cream into her mouth. "Does this involve going someplace I don't want to go and doing something I don't want to do?"

"Nah. This one is easy. It's just outside in the yard."

Juniper told Tori about the ghosts' clues as they finished their ice cream, and then they headed outside.

"Brrr… it's cold out." Juniper rubbed her arms. "Didn't seem this cold last night at midnight."

"I think that was the champagne, June."

Juniper laughed. "Luckily, the cleanup crew hasn't gotten to the decorations. The bucket is still there."

Over by the side of the house, the four-foot-tall gold bucket stood with its fake ice cubes and inflatable champagne bottle.

"This looks like the perfect place to hide a gun!" Juniper plunged her hand into the fake ice, which was really Styrofoam, and rummaged around.

"Be careful. You don't want it to go off!" Tori said. "And don't touch it. It's evidence."

"Good point. We should have put on gloves. Too late now. Get on the other side and help me out." Juniper nodded toward the opposite side of the bucket.

Tori did as told, her face showing concentration as she rummaged around.

"I don't feel anything in here but Styrofoam," she said.

"Me too." Juniper leaned over the edge so she could get to the bottom. She fished and thrashed around, throwing fake ice everywhere and growing more disappointed by the minute.

"I think I've got something!" Tori said. "It doesn't feel like a gun, though…"

Tori pulled her hand out to reveal… a book of matches.

"Matches?" Juniper made a face.

"Well, they do have sulfur on them." Tori handed them to Juniper.

"But none of them have been lit. If he can smell this, his sense of smell must be fantastic." The matches had the familiar black-and-green logo of Rotgut & Ruin, the bar in the less desirable section of town. She'd been to the bar a time or two and happened to know a little secret about the owner. "Do you think this matchbook has anything to do with the murder?"

Tori glanced back into the ice bucket and made a face. "Doubtful."

"But what if the gun *was* in here and then someone took it out? Maybe they dropped the matches by mistake."

"In that case, you shouldn't be getting your fingerprints all over them." Tori glanced around the yard. "But when would someone have come back here to retrieve it? The cops have had the yard blocked off and have been here searching until about an hour ago. So if it was here, someone would have had to take it last night before the yard was blocked off."

"I wonder if the cops checked in here. Maybe they did, and they have the gun now."

"I think you're grasping at straws. How reliable are ghosts? Maybe Jacobi just thought he smelled something. He's pretty old. Sense of smell goes when you are old." Tori crossed her arms over her chest. "Why are you so determined, anyway? Is it because Chalis is one of the suspects, or are you just trying to show up Mallard?"

Juniper sighed. "I *know* Chalis couldn't kill someone, but I've left him several messages, and he hasn't answered. And he did have a beef with Berkshaw. I'm worried Detective McDuck is going to find out about that and see arresting him as a convenient way to close the case."

"I don't think Detective Mallard would just arrest someone if he didn't have evidence."

"Maybe. But I'd love to know what they do have for evidence. Like how close the shooter was. I still haven't ruled out Madison Lane. She was right next to him and hightailed it out of the vicinity pretty quick."

"I guess there's only one way to find out what the cops know," Tori said. "But I doubt Desmond will tell you much."

Juniper held up the matches. "But now, with the ghosts' observations and these matches, I have something to barter with. Maybe I can use my powers of persuasion to get him to trade clues."

CHAPTER NINE

Desmond Mallard looked up from the half-inch-thick folder in his hand and stared at the one woman he'd never expected to come willingly to his office at the precinct. "Ms. Holiday, I appreciate your efforts with this. I do. But you do understand most of what you've given me is hearsay. The rest is likely unusable, as it's just... um... ghostsay."

"But it's all reliable, DuckyMuck. You know my ghosts would never lie about what they saw —and they were there! You weren't, and not for lack of an invite, if you'll recall," Juniper told him.

"Reliable or not, there's no proof. Felicity saw the mayor argue with Mrs. Lane? Great.

Jacobi smelled sulfur. Perfect. Did he see anyone with a smoking gun?"

"So it *was* a gunshot?" Juniper grabbed a sticky note from the corner of his desk and a pen. "What caliber? What type of gun? How far away was the shooter?"

Desmond thought she had surely lost her mind.

"Ms. Holiday. Juniper. Or June. Or Juni—whatever I have to call you to get anything through that thick head of yours…" he said, this close to losing whatever hold he'd had on his temper from the minute he saw her where she shouldn't have been—which was anywhere he was. "This is official police business. A job for the people trained and authorized to look into these things, see? And you're neither of those, so please hear me when I say I cannot discuss this with you."

"Pffft," she said, knocking down his insistence with a wave of her hand. "That's ridiculous, and you know it. Everyone gets that two heads are better than one in a matter like this. You just don't want the second one to be mine."

Swallowing back the reply he really wanted to give her, Desmond counted quietly to three and asked, "Do you remember the night of the party, Ms. Holiday? We spoke. You recall our conversation? The one where I specifically told you to keep your thoughts, feelings, ideas, and hunches in regard to this case to yourself?"

"I do, yes," Juniper assured him. She even backed up her answer with a few nods of her head. "You said it's 'high profile,' and I shouldn't muck around in it, but what do you consider the most wealthy person in Crescent Cove, Detective, if not high profile?"

"A pain in my a—"

"Are you saying I'm not good enough? Is that it? You think because I like my cars fast and my music loud and the decisions I make for myself are often in direct opposition to everyone else, I'm not capable of finding out who killed the mayor? At my house. On my lawn. Among my own friends?"

Too late, Desmond realized he may have stuck his foot so deep in his mouth there'd be no getting out of the lecture she was about to deliver. Unless…

"Absolutely not," he said then motioned with the folder for her to follow him. He led her to a conference room, and once she was inside, he closed the door.

"Look, I know you know what you know, Ms. Holiday. I wouldn't dare to insult your intelligence. Not to your face, anyway," he mumbled at the end. "That's why I'm going to send in one of my associates, Mr. Nichols. He will love speaking with you. Feel free to go over the content of this folder with him."

Tossing the folder onto the table, Desmond turned to leave.

"Even the bit about how Preston Lane was there, and he seemed tense all night? And William Walcroft wanted to get a project approved but the mayor refused?"

He stopped with his hand on the door. He should leave. Now. He knew he should. But then—

"And what about this piece of evidence?" Juniper pulled something out of her pocket and slid it across the table.

"A matchbook from the Rotgut & Ruin? Maybe you have been spending too much time there. That would explain why you keep coming to me with circumstantial evidence."

"They aren't mine, McDuckers. I found

them in the giant ice bucket where Jacobi smelled sulfur."

"And this is related to the murder how?"

"Don't you see? If the killer did hide the gun in there to be retrieved later, then maybe they dropped the matches." Juniper tapped the matchbook with her index finger. "There could be prints on it."

"That proves nothing. Those matches could have gotten there at any time. There is nothing tying them to the murder." Desmond closed his eyes and turned away from the door. "Do you have your cell phone, Ms. Holiday?"

Juniper nodded. He nodded too. "Good. Good. You should take it out now and call your goddaughter, Victoria. Tell her she needs to drive down and collect you."

She made a face at him, some kind of cross between disgust and confusion. "Why would I do that, Duckman? I drove myself here, and I can drive myself home."

"Right. Right," Desmond agreed. "But what you can't do, Ms. Holiday, is get yourself out of jail, which is what you're going to need Victoria to do... if you continue to insist on getting involved in this... this murder case! Do you not realize you could end up getting yourself killed?"

Juniper was already sidling toward the door, the manila file folder in hand. "What I realize is that I'm going to have to do this by myself, just as I suspected. Good day, Duck Boy. You're swimming too shallow to be called a man."

Stunned—though he wasn't sure whether the feeling was due to the insult she'd dealt or the fact that he'd temporarily won—Desmond watched her walk down the hallway and out the front door of the precinct before he realized Nichols had come up beside him and was watching her too.

"Seems like she could have been on to something there, Detective Mallard, sir."

Desmond's piercing look was questioning.

The younger man blushed. "Sorry, sir, but I was in the anteroom off the back of the conference room. Heard every word y'all said. But I could forget if you want me to, sir," he assured him as he held up his hand. "D'you want me to, sir?"

Closing his eyes, Desmond shook his head yet again—something he'd found himself doing much too often lately—ever since his first entanglement with Ms. Juniper Holiday at Halloween, which was months ago. "What I want, Nichols, is for you to do your job so that I can do mine. Is that clear? Do you understand?"

Harvey was already nodding. "Yes, sir. Crystal, sir. I'll just get to it right now."

CHAPTER TEN

Juniper drove past the old Marston mansion on her way home. There was no sign of Chalis. He hadn't answered her texts or calls, either.

She stomped into her foyer, her mind whirling about what to do next. Opening the ginormous coat closet, she almost had a heart attack when Felicity swirled up to her out of the darkness.

"Ack! Give a girl a warning next time," Juniper said.

"You didn't tell me you got a new coat." Felicity huffed.

"Huh?" Juniper looked down. She was wearing the purple Columbia puffer jacket with a faux-fur hood that she'd had for two years now. "I always wear this."

"Not that one." Felicity raised her ghostly arm and pointed toward the far end of the closet. "The one down there."

Juniper squinted into the darkness. The coat closet was more like a coatroom. It was narrow and about twenty feet long with racks on either side. Of course, Juniper and Tori didn't have nearly enough coats to fill it, but the extra room came in handy for parties when dozens of guests had coats to offload. Right now, it was pretty much empty, with a cluster of coats at the far end.

"If you ask me, it's a little much, but what do I know?" Felicity sounded miffed as she floated toward the collection of coats.

Great, that was just what Juniper needed: *two* ghosts that were mad at her. Though Lionel was starting to thaw a bit, she hoped.

Juniper went to the end and browsed through the coats. There was her ski jacket, her leather, her jacket for light rain, for heavy rain, and …

"Oh, you mean this one?" She pulled out a blond mink on a hanger. It was waist length with a furry, real mink face—complete with eyes and teeth—on the collar. "Yech!" Juniper practically dropped it.

"That's what I thought." Felicity swirled in front of her. "So it's not yours?"

"Hardly. You know I always show you my new coats." Juniper had learned years ago that Felicity had a thing for coats.

"Oh. Of course. Sorry I jumped to conclusions. I was in here checking to make sure Anna had cleaned properly after the party. I know she does a good job, but the closet can get so smelly after all the aromas from those coats. All the guests' coats are gone, so I assumed this was yours or Ms. Tori's."

"Well, it's not mine, and Tori doesn't do fur. Someone must have left it." Juniper remembered seeing the guests out. No one was without a coat that she could remember. But had she seen everyone? She hadn't seen Chalis or the blonde. But this jacket seemed sort of old-fashioned for a young woman to wear.

Juniper checked the pockets and the labels in the lining, but there was nothing to indicate who the owner was. She'd hired help to serve and check coats, so she doubted Terrence or Anna would know anything, but maybe she would ask just in case.

She was on her way out of the closet with the jacket when Lionel swirled in from the hall.

"A Chalis McGregor to see you, Mum," Lionel informed her about two seconds before Terrence stuck his head into the room and told her the same thing.

"Thank you, Lionel," Juniper said, hoping this meant that her ghost butler was back to normal now.

"Show him to the library, Terry! And see if Sabrina can spare a second to fix up a charcuterie board. A cheese one! With olives and crackers!"

If she knew Chalis, and she did, he would be snackish. He always was. If he wasn't sipping something, he was eating something. How he managed to maintain a mostly trim figure, she'd never understand. He wasn't particularly athletic, nor did he favor exercise in the least. He must be blessed was all she could figure.

She tucked the fur coat under her arm and headed off to the library to meet her old friend.

CHAPTER ELEVEN

"I got your twenty messages. What gives?" Chalis asked after kissing her on the cheek.

"I missed seeing you at the end of my party and wanted to catch up." Juniper held the coat out. "Do you recognize this?"

Chalis jumped back. "Yech! No! What is that?"

"Mink coat. I thought maybe it belonged to the woman in the fuchsia dress that you disappeared with." Juniper wiggled her eyebrows.

"Umm. No. She had a Canada Goose jacket. And we didn't disappear." Chalis grinned with a sparkle in his eye. "We gave our statements to the police and took our private party elsewhere."

"Sounds like you've been busy." Juniper felt better about the missed calls and guilty for having the slightest suspicion of Chalis. Even though they hadn't seen each other in years, she trusted him implicitly. They had too much history. Even if he was connected to *him*.

She still couldn't bring herself to say his name or even think it. One day, she might move on from him, but that day was clearly not today.

"Is that why you've been leaving me all those messages? To find out the sordid details of my love life?" Chalis teased.

"Hardly. I don't want to learn anything that might scare me. I just wanted to catch up since we didn't get a chance to do that at the party."

Chalis nodded. "Me too. Did you know it's almost impossible to get in here without a dozen reporters barking questions at you and shoving things in your face?"

Juniper rolled her eyes and slumped onto the cushions of the settee across from Chalis. "Yes. They're like roaches. They won't go away no matter how many times you spray 'em."

A grin broke across Chalis's face. "I thought

that was you I saw wielding the water hose yesterday."

"I told them to clear out or suffer the consequences. They didn't listen." She sighed. "I guess it didn't work too well, though, if they're back like you said."

"Might be different ones."

She snorted. "I doubt it."

They chatted about different things for a few minutes, then Sabrina came in with a cart full of goodies that she looked only too happy to serve. Juniper smiled to herself as she watched the young woman happily explain the different ways she'd experimented with mashed potatoes to get them to the perfect consistency every time without fail. Chalis listened eagerly. When it came to food, he was always interested.

Finally, Sabrina left them to eat, and after Chalis had put away half the spread on his own, he looked to her and said, "So you're still into planning parties, I see."

She frowned and pointed at the tray. "This is hardly a party, Chalis."

He gave her a look. "I meant the New Year's party."

"Oh. Right. I guess you could say that," she said with a chuckle.

"You've always been good at it."

"It's my calling, I'm sure of it."

"And you know what they say: what you're doing on New Year's, you'll be doing for the rest of the year."

For some reason, hearing that made Juniper deflate. Suddenly, she felt exhausted. Someone had lost their life that night, and her life hadn't been the same since Halloween, filled with murder and thieves, and it was just… just… a giant mess.

Suddenly, she found herself lamenting her woes since Halloween to one of her oldest friends in the world, but by the time she was done unloading, she felt a little better. She hadn't realized how much everything had started to weigh on her until she vomited all her feelings on Chalis—who took it like a champ, mind you. He'd always been a good listener, though. He'd helped her through more than one problem over the years, including the deaths of two of their dearest friends in the world—Laura and Nathaniel Cooper, Victoria's parents.

They were killed in a car accident. It wasn't

murder, but Juniper had longed to pin it on someone back then. She needed someone to blame, needed to hear something other than "sometimes these things just happen." Maybe that was why she kept making trouble for Detective Waddlebutt. She wanted to give the victims' families closure that she hadn't felt she'd had once upon a time.

Juniper, never one to dwell on her own problems, changed the subject to something happier. "You're a good friend to talk to. I'm glad you might be moving back. How is that going, anyway?"

Chalis's expression darkened, reminding Juniper of the animosity between him and the late mayor. "Oh, you know. I've had to jump through hoops and spend lots of time at city hall."

"But you're making progress?"

"You know how stubborn Berkshaw could be." Chalis glanced out the window. "But maybe things are looking up."

Hopefully, he wasn't saying that because he would benefit from Berkshaw's death. Chalis wasn't the only one who would benefit, though.

"I was wondering, if you've been spending

time at city hall, maybe you saw something that might help with the case. I mean, someone had a motive to kill Berkshaw."

"Motive? You mean like a project he was getting in the way of or something?" Chalis screwed up his face and thought about it. "Well, there was something odd one time. I was flirting with one of the women there when Madison Lane came out of his office and slammed the door. She was mad as anything. But as soon as she saw me looking at her, she tried to pretend that she was just there on some sort of business."

"Really? That's odd. Berkshaw did have that effect on people, though."

"Yeah, except that wasn't the only time. One other time, I heard them yelling at each other."

"Oh? Was Preston there too?" Maybe Madison and Preston had a project that the mayor was holding up. That would explain why Preston looked bothered by something at the party.

Chalis shook his head. "Nope. Just Madison."

"Did you ever see William Walcroft argue

with him? I know he had a project the mayor was refusing to fund."

"Nope. Just Madison."

That was certainly interesting. Why was Madison arguing with the mayor so much, and was she mad enough to kill him?

"Detective Mallard wants to do another search of the property," Harvey Nichols told Tori the following afternoon.

"Oh?" Tori raised a brow. "Did something Juniper say yesterday sink in?"

"Not sure, but I think he was a little afraid something wasn't right after Ms. Holiday left the precinct yesterday, you know? 'Cause she left too quietly and all that." He shook his head. A smile lingered on his lips. "That godmother of yours, she sure is something, Ms. Victoria."

"She's definitely something, Detective Nichols. Just most of us haven't yet figured out what," Tori told him. Then, she called through the lower portion of the house, "Juniper! June, the detectives are here!"

Down the hall in the card room, Juniper sighed. She had stacks and piles of Valentine's Day cards and decorations spread all over the red-felted billiards table, the chessboard in the corner, and the poker table too. Loki was busy pushing the cards off the table while Ludo sat below, ready to swat them around the room. Finn was busy lying on top of whatever project she happened to be working on at any given moment.

She was in the middle of deciding on a theme of sorts for her next holiday celebration, and she wasn't in the mood for... whatever the detectives had in mind. "Tell them I'm busy," she called back. "Duckbuster and his little waddlers can come back later. Preferably in some other lifetime far in the future."

Not only wasn't she in the mood for chitchat, she was still figuratively gnawing at her fingernails over her conversation with Chalis. He'd purposely avoided her question about his house project. And when he'd mentioned things might be looking up, she couldn't help but wonder if that was because his biggest roadblock, Mayor Berkshaw, had been eliminated.

"June, you know they're not going to go away that easily," Tori said from the doorway.

Juniper didn't even look up from the stacks of invitations she was going through. "Let them do whatever they want, Tori. I don't have time to talk to them. You handle it."

Her brow arched high, Tori said, "Fine."

She leaned back into the hallway and yelled, "Yo, Duckman! She's back here at the billiards table. You wanna go around?"

"Oh, good grief!" Juniper mumbled. "What'd you go and do that for, Tor? You know he just wants to aggravate me about this murdered mayor thing. He wants to know what I know while telling me I can't get involved."

She picked up a stack of invites and headed directly for her goddaughter. She stopped. "Let the little platypus do his own investigating. I have troubles of my own to deal with."

"And those would be?" Desmond Mallard asked from behind Tori's shoulder. He'd come down the hallway while Juniper was explaining to Tori why she wasn't answering to the local detectives today, and now, there he was.

"There's no avoiding you today, is there?"

Desmond shook his head. "Not if you want me to leave, and I'm sure you do—as quickly as possible—so we might as well get this done."

"What do you want, Duckboy? I'm trying to organize for Valentine's Day and really don't have time."

But she hadn't been doing any organizing, either. Not really. She'd been angsting over Chalis and the possible murder charge that might be hanging over his head. In fact, she'd obsessed over it so much, she'd barely slept a wink last night—not that she'd tell the detective that bit. She certainly wasn't going to be the one to tell McDuck about the problems between Berkshaw and Chalis. He was the detective. Let him figure that out on his own.

"I'd like to take another sweep through the yard for the gun. Maybe even look in that giant ice bucket you mentioned," Mallard said as Loki trotted over to sniff his shoes. Finn had retreated to the back of the room and was glaring at Mallard—a good judge of character, no doubt.

"Aha! So you do think that's related." Juniper felt somewhat vindicated and also filed away the fact that this meant that they hadn't found the gun yet. "You may search wherever you like."

"That was easy," Mallard said. "Something must be getting to you. I presume it must be about the murder. Is there something I should know, Ms. Holiday?"

Juniper looked at him as if he'd grown three new heads. "Yes! Tons. All the things I tried to bring to your attention yesterday, as a matter of fact. How do you do it, Detective? How do you personally take all the strings and raveled threads and put all the correct strands together?"

Desmond held his silence for a moment, though he never broke eye contact with her. Finally, he said, "It isn't easy—even for me. I've had to investigate some stomach-twisting, heart-wrenching scenarios, Ms. Holiday, and the best way I've found to deal with it when one's emotions are too involved is to put all the noise, the clutter, the nonsense aside and weigh nothing but the facts."

As soon as he finished talking, he turned around and left her alone again, no further questions asked. Juniper's mouth almost fell open in shock. "Well, I never!"

And she hadn't, not once. She'd been so caught up in worry over whether or not Chalis was guilty, whether or not people thought her mansion was cursed, whether or not people would stop judging her by her outward appearances, and so on and so forth, she'd never really considered doing what the detective told her— just push it all aside and only look at the facts.

Now that she had, well… Juniper dropped the invitations on a nearby table and struck out for her office. She'd need pen and paper for this, for sure. As she slid the chair underneath the desk as far as it would go with her in it, she shook her head in mild disbelief. The detective had finally said something that made sense, and bless her if she wasn't going to take his advice and do it.

The mansion practically pulsed with sound. During moments of intense concentration, Juniper listened to music at full blast, which was not unlike her usual day-to-day activity, except that she didn't dance and sing along. No, she was too busy laying out just the facts, like the Duckster said—and God help anyone (Tori) if they (she) mentioned anything about her taking his advice.

Everyone in the estate was used to the noise, so it didn't bother them, not even Tori, who was up to her eyeballs writing her latest Victorian Gothic. Of course, Tori wasn't averse to slipping on noise-canceling headphones if she needed to, either.

But Juniper wasn't thinking about any of that. She was only focused on the facts about the murder. She knew Chalis didn't do it, and she wanted to figure out who did before Mallard added him to the suspect list. She was sure the killer had a personal motivation, so proving what that motivation was would help calm people's nerves about her parties being cursed.

A knock sounded at her door, the noise jarring her from her concentration. Frowning, she glared at the door and yelled, "What?"

"You okay in there?" came Tori's voice, muffled through the thick wood.

"Yes, I'm fine. Tori, open the door. You know I can't hear you through that thing."

"And yet you heard my question just fine," Tori said, opening the door wide. She walked over to Juniper's desk and leaned against it. "The music stopped. We weren't sure if it was on purpose or if you'd died in here and were trying to communicate via radio waves."

"I think I'd use something other than silence to communicate I was dead, Tor."

"It wouldn't work the same," Tori said, shaking her head. "Music is your thing. No music, especially after days of it, is very telling."

Juniper leaned back in her chair and regarded Tori for a moment. "Sometimes quiet is needed."

"Ha! With you? Never. If you're ever quiet, something is up."

Juniper smiled. "You got me all figured out, don't you?"

Tori tilted her head. "That's a trick question, and we both know it. I know you pretty well, I'd say, but having you all figured out is a whole other monster. One I don't feel like poking right now."

A chuckle fell from Juniper's lips. "Not that brave yet?"

"Oh, I'm plenty brave. I just don't feel like absorbing that much information right now. I've got enough of other people's lives floating around in my head all the time with my characters—and they're made up. The brain cramp I'd get from you is deterrent enough to keep me from provoking the beast, thanks."

That made Juniper laugh, then she said, "So is that the only reason you came in here? To make sure I was still alive and hadn't given up the ghost yet?"

"Pretty much," Tori said, shrugging one

shoulder. "Well, that, and Sabrina said to tell you you've got to come taste the potato salad. She adjusted the recipe slightly and wants to know what you think."

"She's ruined it is what she's done," Jacobi bemoaned as he floated in from the ceiling.

Juniper snorted. "Jackie-boy, you say she ruins everything," she said as she got up and followed Tori from the room.

"What's he whining about?" Tori asked, looking over her shoulder at Juniper, her eyes searching the empty space around her godmother for a spirit she would probably never see.

If she had to go the way the Duckman had, Juniper hoped she never saw them. She could deal with being the only one besides Desmond who could see the mansion's spirits. She waved her hand and answered Tori's question. "What he always whines about. He thinks Sabrina ruined the tater salad."

"Can he taste anything?"

A haughty sniff was Jacobi's answer, which Tori couldn't hear. But Juniper could, and it made her laugh. "No, he can't, but he can smell pretty good," she answered for him. "He just thinks anything deviating from what he's used to is bad. He's an old codger stuck in his ways."

Jacobi narrowed ghostly eyes at Juniper and said some things that didn't bear repeating in polite company. Not that Juniper was polite, but she didn't think Tori wanted to hear it, as it was rather colorful and on this side of offensive, so she kept it to herself, laughing inside at Jacobi's obvious pique.

Heading into the kitchen, Sabrina was ready with a spoonful of potatoes. "I tweaked the mustard-to-pickle juice ratio. What do you think?"

Juniper leaned in and took a bite, her eyes rolling back in her head a second later as the flavors burst on her tongue. "My goodness, Sab. This is perfect."

Sabrina beamed. "Really?"

"Oh, absolutely," Juniper said. "Tori, you taste it."

Tori did and had much the same reaction as Juniper.

"What else you got cooked up?" Juniper asked, her eyes scanning the countertop for other dishes.

Sabrina ended up serving them plates of

fried green beans, fried chicken, her improved potato salad, biscuits fresh from the oven, and a big ol' slice of chocolate cake on the side.

Juniper and Tori took their plates to the dining room and ate there.

"So what were you doing while you were holed up in your study these last few days, anyway?" Tori asked around a mouthful of food.

"Laying out the facts," Juniper said.

Tori arched a brow. "Really?"

Juniper gave a nod. "Yep. I'll show you in a bit if you want, but I think I've got most of the necessary stuff down so I can focus on solving the murder. I'm a thousand percent determined to save Chalis's behind whether he wants me to or not."

"You just can't let this lie, can you?" Tori asked, shaking her head.

"Nope," Juniper said, popping the *p*.

"So what's your next step?"

"I'm going to pay a little visit to Wanda over at the town hall. She probably knows everything about the mayor's sordid business, and I want to see what I can get out of her."

"Sounds like you are planning on sticking your nose in deep this time," Tori said.

"People keep falling dead around me, and until they stop, I'm going to stick my nose in all the places I shouldn't. If your befeathered beau has a problem with it, that's just tough cookies."

Tori shook her head again, but she was smiling. "You're going to get into so much trouble, Juniper."

Juniper winked. "Sweetheart, that's my middle name."

Juniper knew that the way to get people to talk was to bribe them with food, so she stopped by Dusty Buns Bakery on her way to the town hall and picked up a baker's dozen of Sprinky Dinks.

Wanda Masters was the receptionist at the town hall. She was in her midfifties with bright-red hair and a pleasantly plump appearance. Her face lit up when Juniper slid the box of Sprinky Dinks onto her desk.

"That's so nice of you." Wanda's hand hovered over the open box as she selected one. Then her eyes narrowed as she looked up at Juniper. "What are you up to?"

Juniper laughed as if she were the last

person in the world that would be up to some-thing. "I just wanted to spread some cheer. It must be a bit depressing here ever since… you know." Juniper didn't want to bring Wanda down by mentioning the word "murder."

Wanda took a bite of her donut, and Juniper selected one for herself. She would have offered them around, but no one else was there. The place was actually a little eerie. Her footsteps echoing on the marble tile as she walked toward the office had sounded hollow, and the large receptionist room was strangely quiet. All the better to get gossip out of Wanda, though.

Wanda glanced over at the mayor's office. "Actually, it's kind of nice. Quiet. The vice mayor is having the office renovated to her liking."

"She is?" Juniper hadn't considered Sally Grover, the vice mayor, as a suspect. Would she kill to get the position of power? "She must have been excited to move up the ladder."

"You'd think, but she's actually upset. Liked her position because she didn't have to do much. Now she has inherited all his projects, and according to her, it's a mess." Wanda took a large bite of the donut.

Juniper crossed Sally off the suspect list. "I heard a lot of people were having trouble getting their projects through."

"Not everybody. There's been a few people, though. Things have been volatile here."

"You don't say." Juniper grabbed a chair from the corner and scooted it close to Wanda. "I heard he'd been making some enemies in that department. And that he'd been very friendly in others."

"Very friendly? What's that mean?" Wanda shoved the last of her donut into her mouth and eyed the box.

Juniper gestured for her to take another as she leaned forward and whispered. "I heard he was having an affair."

Wanda's gaze jerked from the donuts to Juniper, her eyes registering disbelief. "The mayor? With who?"

That was odd because Juniper figured if the mayor was carrying on, Wanda would know. "I'm not sure, but Madison Lane comes to mind. I heard from the grapevine that she was here arguing with the mayor on more than one occasion. Perhaps a lovers' quarrel?"

Wanda made a face, her eyes cutting over to

the door to the mayor's office. "She did argue with him several times, but I thought it was over a project."

"But you aren't certain?"

"Well, I don't know. I mean, where would they have an affair… in his office?" Wanda shook her head. "No, I didn't suspect that at all."

"Were there any other women the mayor seemed overly friendly with?" Juniper asked.

Wanda thought about it while chewing. "I don't think so."

"Did he argue with other people?"

Wanda nodded. "Plenty of them. Like Chalis McGregor. He wanted to renovate that old mansion. I'm still not sure why Mayor Berkshaw was so against it. Would be an improvement if you ask me. I got the impression they didn't like each other much."

Juniper hoped Wanda didn't mention that to the police. Juniper didn't know if the police had already interviewed her, but it might be a good idea to get Wanda thinking about other people the mayor was causing problems for. "What about Preston Lane?"

Wanda nodded. "Yep, he had some arguments with the mayor. But not recently. Recently, it was mostly the wife."

"And William Walcroft?"

"William? No, he didn't argue with Berkshaw."

"He didn't? His wife said he had some project he wanted pushed through, and Berkshaw was holding it up."

Wanda frowned. "Project? I don't think so."

"Are you sure?"

"Of course I'm sure. I do all the paperwork and filing." Wanda swiveled her chair to face her computer and started typing. "I'll just double-check."

Juniper munched her donut while Wanda's fingers clacked over the keys. After a few minutes of searching, she spun back to face Juniper. "Nope. There's one with Preston Lane's name on it but no project by William Walcroft. Though I did hear that he's getting a divorce."

"A divorce? No. They were both at my party the other night." Juniper was surprised.

Wanda shrugged. "I heard it was sudden. One never knows what other people have going on."

That was interesting. They had seemed so

"together" at her party. And Donna had specifically said he was looking for the mayor, hoping to talk to him about a project. Maybe William and the mayor were just in the talking stage. Either way, it appeared she'd tapped her resources here. Madison Lane was looking a bit guilty, but so was Chalis.

Juniper had to do something to push the other suspects to the forefront of the police investigation, but Ducky-doo wouldn't listen to her. She was going to have to send another concerned citizen that had information on the case to him, and she knew exactly who that citizen was.

Fedora took a sip of her hazelnut latte, making cooing noises down in her throat as she did so. "Oh, my word! I forget how good the java is here at the Witch-Roast. I love it every single time. Thanks for bringing me here, Juni. I'll owe ya one."

"Yeah, one you're about to pay up on right now, Fedora Layhee. You're the one that said something about Madison Lane and the mayor having an affair, and now you're going to tell me how you learned this," Juniper told her.

Fedora's brow creased. "Ulterior motives? Juni, sweets, this isn't what I was expecting from you. Usually, you cajole such information out of me a little at a time…"

"Time is what I don't have, Dori. Not now. This time, the coffee will have to suffice. See, I'm worried about Chalis looking guilty here. He really wanted that house down the street from us, you know? But the mayor kept coming up with reasons that he couldn't have it."

Fedora took another sip. "Are you sure it was the mayor doing that? I mean, why would he? There are plenty of other bigger fish he could fry on the grate of…"

"Fedora, Chalis told me. It was Mayor Berkshaw," Juniper insisted. "Now, tell me how you heard about Madison Lane spending her free time with the mayor. Please."

"Free time, work time, playtime… anytime," Fedora said, then she made a noise that didn't sound very ladylike. "That woman was all up in the mayor's business."

Juniper latched onto those words like a piranha. "You saw them? You saw Madison Lane with Mayor Berkshaw? Personally?"

"No, no…" Fedora put her hand on the edge of the table and pushed back a bit. If they'd been in chairs, she might have gone sprawling backward a foot or two. As it was, they were seated at a booth, so luckily, she stayed where she was. "Not me, Juniper, but I'm also not at liberty to say who I got the information from."

It was Juniper's time to huff an unladylike snort. "You're already repeating it. Now I need to know the source."

"You're not dragging me into this," she said, shaking her head from side to side while she fiddled with the rim of her cup. "We could get arrested, you know. For aiding and abetting or—or—What's that other one?" She snapped her fingers. "Obstructing justice."

"What?" Juniper's eyes narrowed in confusion. "How in the world could being specific about the facts of a matter be considered obstruction?"

"You know how Detective Mallard is." She shrugged then glanced up at the other woman from beneath her lashes. "Tori already told me he specifically ordered you to stay out of this case, June. I think he may be worried about you."

Juniper's back went straight. "Nobody orders me, Dori. Not Tori, not you, and most certainly not the Dastardly Duck. I'm my own woman, fully capable of handling myself. I always accept responsibility for my part in things when it's warranted. But, Dori—Chalis looks guilty, and I know he couldn't have killed the mayor, so we need to help point the investigation in another direction."

"What are you going to do if Chalis *is* the one who killed the mayor, June? It's not like you're going to be able to keep him out of jail, because we were all there. We all can say we know without a doubt there was no fight, so Chal can't claim self-defense," Fedora pointed out.

Juniper shook her head. "No, no, Fedora. He's not guilty. I know Chalis, and there's no way you could convince me he did this horrible thing. And now that you mention Madison and the mayor, I wonder if Preston knew. He seemed like something was bothering him. What if he found out about his wife and the mayor?"

"Then he could be a suspect? Wouldn't be the first husband to shoot his wife's lover."

Juniper paused and took a long drink from her own cup. "Dora. Dori-dear. Look. There are a lot of suspects, but what if the killer knows what was going on between the mayor and Chalis and tries to pin this on him?"

Fedora gave her a look. "If he's not guilty, then he has nothing to worry about. I'm sure Detective Mallard will get to the bottom of it and find the real killer."

After a long look at Fedora, Juniper reached for her purse and rummaged inside until she took out her cell phone. She slid screens with her index finger then pressed a button. "Detective Mallard, please."

To Fedora's surprise, she must have been put right through because she blew off normal greetings and went straight to the point. "Detective, I'm with a friend who has some information that might be helpful in the mayor's murder investigation."

"... names, Ms. Holiday," Fedora heard the detective say.

"Fedora Layhee. Start with her. She will be happy to tell you whatever you need to know."

Juniper ended the call without saying goodbye. She put her phone back in her purse and waved away Fedora's wide-eyed look. "Oh, stop, Dori. He won't hurt ya. Just... tell him all the things you wouldn't tell me just now."

CHAPTER SIXTEEN

Desmond regarded Fedora with a scrutinizing gaze. Their paths had not crossed often, the last time that he could remember being at Juniper's Thanksgiving party. He felt his eye start to twitch at the thought and forced himself not to react. Three months. Juniper Holiday and her shenanigans had been the cause of his migraines for three months.

If he had known then…

Fedora fidgeted in her seat, fiddling with her fingers and looking everywhere but at him. She even worried at her bottom lip.

"Are you afraid of me, Mrs. Layhee?"

If it was possible for a person to jump a foot

sitting down, she did, the chair she was seated in giving a creak at the sudden motion. Her hand fluttered to her chest. "Goodness, Detective, you gave me a fright! Warn a lady next time you're going to blurt something out after staring at me, please."

Desmond almost cracked a smile. "You didn't answer my question."

Fedora blinked owlishly. "What did you ask me?"

Desmond sighed and flicked his fingers in a dismissive gesture. "Never mind. Mrs. Layhee, Ms. Holiday tells me you have information that may be helpful to this case. Is that true?"

Fedora's lips puckered. "That depends on what you want to know, Detective."

"Names, Mrs. Layhee. I want to know how you came by the knowledge of the accusation that Mrs. Lane was having an affair with Mayor Berkshaw. Who told you?"

Fedora fluttered her lashes. "Oh, no. I couldn't say, Detective. I was sworn to silence. Juni only got it out of me because she can do that to people, you know? Get them to talk when they didn't mean to. I don't know how she does it. I've been trying to figure it out for years, but all I manage is to spill secrets that are best left kept quiet."

Desmond leaned forward, resting his arms atop his desk. "You wouldn't like it in jail, Fedora. And obstruction—"

"It was Iphigenia Gregorovitch. She told me a cousin of hers, who is very close to someone that works at the mayor's mansion, told her that"—she glanced around her to make sure they were alone then leaned close like she was imparting a great secret—"there was an illicit affair going on."

Desmond looked up from his notepad, where he'd been taking down everything Fedora had said. "And did she say it was with Madison Lane?"

"Err, well, no. I mean she didn't want to be crass and name names, but I saw Madison and the mayor whispering together at the New Year's Eve party."

"Uh-huh. And wasn't Madison standing beside the mayor when he was shot?"

"Yes! See? She was standing right there beside him!"

"Well, then she can't be the killer. The mayor was shot from at least twenty feet away."

"Oh. Well. That does seem to indicate she is innocent." Fedora gnawed her bottom lip. "So do you think Preston did it, then? Maybe he found out and was jealous?"

Detective Mallard sat back and crossed his arms over his chest. "We're investigating all suspects, Mrs. Layhee. Now, is there anything else you'd like to tell me?"

Fedora puckered up her lips again, tilting her head to the side and tapping her cheek as she thought. "Well... I did speak to the mayor's widow."

"When?" Desmond leaned forward and focused on his notepad once again, pen at the ready.

"It was just yesterday," Fedora said.

"And what did the two of you discuss?"

"Oh, I gave her my condolences for her loss. Losing a husband isn't easy."

Desmond looked up, his brows low. "I thought your husband was still alive?"

"Oh, he is," Fedora said, nodding her head. "Bernard is very much alive and kicking, Detective. I just meant that losing someone so close to you, especially a spouse, well, that's a special sort of pain, you know."

"I wouldn't."

Fedora's brow crinkled, her expression indicating his answer had surprised her. He didn't see the need to go into details, so he kept to the business at hand. "Did she seem to indicate that she knew her husband was having an affair?"

"Oh, no, no. Definitely not."

"What makes you so certain, Mrs. Layhee? Perhaps Mrs. Berkshaw was the one to pull the trigger and end her husband's life. Jealousy does funny things to people."

"I don't think so, Detective… what does Juni call you? Waddlebutt?"

Desmond's expression flattened at the mention of Juniper Holiday and but one of many bastardizations of his surname she had taken to using. "I'll thank you to not call me that, Mrs. Layhee," he warned.

Fedora flushed bright red. "Oh dear. I crossed a line, didn't I? I do apologize, Detective Mallard. It's just that when Juni says it, it sounds so fun. Rolls right off the tongue. Waaaddlebutt," she enunciated slowly as though to demonstrate.

"Holding cell," he enunciated right back.

"My apologies, Detective Mallard. I'll stick to that one."

"Thank you." He lowered his head once more. "Now, why do you think Mrs. Berkshaw is innocent?"

"She was so distraught. She didn't stop crying the whole time I was talking to her." Fedora shook her head. "No, I just can't picture her being the killer. Besides, wasn't she coming back from the airport? The timing doesn't work."

Desmond couldn't help but wonder if Juniper had been feeding Fedora clues. Of course she had. The information about Susan Berkshaw being on her way back from the airport must have come straight from Juniper.

Realizing where his thoughts had gone, Desmond barely caught himself from rolling his eyes—something he had never done prior to becoming acquainted with that dratted woman—and said to Fedora, "Thank you for your time, Mrs. Layhee. You may go now. I will call you should I need anything else."

"Of course, Detective," Fedora said, getting up to leave. She paused with her hand on the door and looked back at him over her shoulder.

"You know, you're not nearly as prickly as Juniper says you are."

That startled a laugh out of Desmond, which he tried to disguise as a cough, and he waved Fedora away before she tried to help him.

Alone, Desmond gave into the laughter, wondering all the while what had gotten into him.

"*D*id anyone come to claim the coat?" Juniper asked when she got home.

Terence glanced at the coat, which was draped over a chair, and made a face. "Sorry, mum. No one has come for it."

Juniper stared at the coat as Terence walked off. Why would someone leave a coat? It made no sense because it had been cold out. Could it be a clue? Or were they just so upset at the murder that they rushed out so quickly after talking to the police that they forgot all about it? It wasn't the sort of coat one wore every day, so maybe they didn't even realize they'd left it.

Her phone chirped. It was Fedora.

"Madison Lane didn't do it," Fedora said.

"How do you know that?"

"I just talked to your Duckman. The mayor was shot from a distance, and Madison was standing right next to him, so she's not the killer. I just hope Chalis can prove he wasn't on the side of the house."

"Me too. Thanks for calling, and thanks for talking to the police."

"You owe me one." Fedora hung up, and Juniper made her way to her office and sat behind the desk, which Sabrina had just loaded up with a smorgasbord of snacks.

Juniper munched on a celery stick as she mentally crossed Madison off her suspect list and moved Preston Lane up. If he knew about the affair, he would have the strongest motive.

And what about William Walcroft? Something about the fact that there was no project on record didn't sit right. His wife had said he had to visit the mayor at home. Could they have had something shady going on? And what about the divorce? Juniper tried to picture Donna Walcroft with the mayor. Maybe it was she having the affair, and she lied to Juniper about a project to throw her off track. Then there was the mysterious woman in the silver dress. Maybe she was the one having the affair with the mayor.

Her eyes fell on the matchbook from Rotgut & Ruin. Mallard didn't think it had anything to do with the murder, but Jacobi had smelled the sulfur at the giant ice bucket, and the matches had been in there. That was a pretty big coincidence. So if the killer dropped the matches by mistake when they were hiding or retrieving the gun, then a visit to Rotgut & Ruin was in order later today. Theodosius, the owner, was usually up on town gossip. He might know something.

Lionel appeared through the bookcase. "Mr. McGregor is here to see you."

He floated off just before Chalis entered the office. At least he had resumed his butler duties. Hopefully, he'd forgiven Juniper for her earlier slight.

"Chalis!" Juniper kissed the air beside his cheek then grabbed both his shoulders to balance herself as she leaned back to give him a once-over. "Twice since the party you're at my house? Are you well? Is something wrong?"

"As a matter of fact, there might be," he said. Shaking her hands free from his shoulders, he straightened then peered at her quizzically.

"Fedora is worried about you, June. Tori too. I'm told you've been putting in an awful lot of unnecessary time on this murder."

"I wouldn't say it's unnecessary—"

"Let the police detectives do their jobs, sweets. That's what they live and die for, you know," he told her then walked around her to sample the snacks on her desk. He picked up an olive-, cheese-, and cherry-stacked sword pick, swiped the contents into his mouth, chewed for a sec, then said, "Tori said you thought I might be on the suspect list?"

Her expression one of angst and misery, Juniper nodded. "I don't think you did it, of course, but Detective McDuck might. I mean, the mayor was trying to ruin your future plans here."

Chalis blinked several times in rapid succession. "Sure, but *moi*? A murderer?"

He flopped down on her sofa, propped his feet on the low coffee table, then crossed them before turning to give her the stink eye again in an overly dramatic fashion. He seriously looked wounded. "You're supposed to be my friend, Juniper Holiday. You're supposed to love me."

Juniper arched a brow. She recognized this

particular bit of flimflammery. He was trying to make her feel guilty for worrying about him. Well, she had too much love for him, in fact, to do anything else. "Chalis, I already said that I didn't think you did it."

"Well, you're right, because everything was already approved. Days before your party, even. I was just waiting for the official letter to come in the mail before I told you."

"Whaaat?" Juniper's genuine surprise showed on her face. "That's great! But why didn't you say something before?"

He shrugged. "I wanted it to be a surprise, and like I said, I was waiting for it to be official. I came to a verbal agreement with Berkshaw a few days before your party, but I didn't trust him not to go back on that. Luckily, he signed the paperwork before he died, and it came in the mail yesterday."

He reached into his coat with the other hand and pulled out a thick packet of folded paper. "Have a look."

Juniper unfolded the papers and grinned. "The deed with no restrictions."

Chalis nodded. "Which is what Mr. Berkshaw and I butted heads over. He wanted to condemn the property and turn it over to the town. I had to prove that I had a feasible plan to make it habitable again."

"We are neighbors!" Juniper's grin hadn't dissipated one whit.

She refolded the papers and swatted him with the stack, which he caught and put back into his pocket. "Yes, we are. Now you can annoy me with your fast car and loud music, and I can annoy you by eating all your food." As if to illustrate, Chalis got up and started picking at the snacks on her desk again.

Juniper leaned her hip against the corner of her desk and shook her head. "This is such a relief. I was afraid Marty McDuck would throw you in jail."

"You know I have no gun, which means I couldn't have shot the mayor because"—he spread his hands wide—"no weapon."

Juniper nodded. "Yes, I know, but things could have changed over the years."

Chalis held up a hand. "No gun. The deed went through before your party, so no motive. I'm free and clear."

"All right. All right. There's no way you could have done it. And if you didn't, and

Fedora said Mallard told her that there's no way the wife did it, there is only one other person it could have been."

"Preston Lane," Chalis said.

"Exactly! Now all I have to do is convince the Duckster to check him out. See what he can find, since he keeps telling me to stay out of things. Can you believe that? Dori thinks that nutster is worried about me, worried I might get myself hurt."

"You? In danger?" Chalis's eyes went wide, then his lips screwed up all funny-like, and he shook his head from side to side. "No, not you. Not in a million years. Doesn't he know you're supernatural?"

Juniper grinned when he amended, "Well, maybe super but probably not natural."

CHAPTER EIGHTEEN

Her vigor restored after determining Chalis was not the killer, and with a new lead to focus on, Juniper decided it was time to pull out the big guns. She did want to talk to Theodosius down at Rotgut & Ruin, but that didn't open for a few hours yet. In the meantime, she needed to talk to Detective Mallard about Preston Lane. But how? She couldn't go to his office again. She'd have to get him to come to her somehow. Perhaps, if she invited him for coffee…

She'd have to invite him to the mansion, of course. It wouldn't be as easy, she didn't think, to get him to listen to her if they were in public, though she knew he was partial to the brew at the WitchRoast Café. But Sabrina could make a fantastic pour, one that not even Jacobi could complain about—mainly because watching her grind the beans, measure out the correct amount, and apply the science of exact timing to boiling water and coffee grounds fascinated him.

Juniper was fascinated as well. Not only with Sabrina's coffee-making skills but her wizardry with food. She'd suggested more than once that Sabrina should open her own restaurant, but Sabrina nixed the idea before it could go too far, stating firmly that she was perfectly fine right where she was, thank you very much. Not wanting to push too much, Juniper didn't press the matter very often, as she didn't want to run her off. She knew if Sabrina felt pressured, she would pack up and leave without another thought.

She was like her mother in that way. And by some stroke of luck, that was why Seraphina was off in France right now, living her dream of being a pastry chef. Because someone (not Juniper) kept telling her to turn her passion for creating things into a career. How making pottery turned into cake baking was beyond

Juniper's understanding, but whatever works, baby!

To lay her trap for the detective, and yes, it was very much a trap, Juniper sent an invitation to Mally-Walley under the guise of it being from Tori. She had, of course, sort of notified Tori of her deception. Tori had been deep into her writing and merely waved it away, so Juniper figured she was in the clear. Anyway, the invitation had been sent and responded to in the affirmative, the front parlor had been prepared, its table laden with finger foods that would pair perfectly with the coffee Sabrina would serve soon, and all Juniper had to do was wait.

A quick glance at her watch revealed the time was nigh, and no sooner did she look than the door opened and Terrence admitted one Desmond Mallard into the room.

Where Juniper sat.

Alone.

She saw the moment he realized he'd been had and prepared to hold the line.

"I'm leaving," he said and started to back out of the room, hand on the doorknob to close it on his way, but Juniper stopped him.

"No, you're not. You're going to sit down

and eat this delicious food Sabrina prepared specifically for us, then you're going to drink the coffee she made, and finally, you're going to listen to what I have to say."

"Ms. Holiday," Desmond began rigidly, "in case you have failed to notice, I am a full-grown man who does not have to answer to you for any reason whatsoever."

Juniper arched her brow. "You're really going to turn down food?"

Desmond stared at her, his gaze practically boring holes into her very soul.

"I'm not hungry."

His stomach growled.

Juniper grinned. "Sit down, Detective," she said, pointing at the vacant seat across from her. "I promise nothing bad is going to happen to you. I only want to talk."

"You'll forgive me if I'm hesitant to partake of any liquid libation you have to offer," he said, making his way over to the empty seat. Juniper had to bite her tongue to keep from pointing out how easily he had changed his mind. "You remember what happened last time."

"That was a fluke," Juniper said. "And it wasn't the coffee itself. Someone put something in it. This time, Sabrina will prepare the coffee right in front of us, so you will know if there's any funny business going on, which there isn't. Besides, what's the worst that can happen, Detective? You die? Again? Pssh! We fixed you then, we'll fix you again."

Desmond regarded her from beneath lowered brows. "There's no guarantee it will work a second time, whatever you did to me."

"I'll let Quincy tell you about it since he was the one who saved you. Now, here's what I called you here for…"

And she proceeded to lay out all the facts for him as they ate. She would only be surprised that he listened to her later, when she had time to think about this almost-pleasant moment between them.

"And that is why I believe Preston Lane is your guy, Duckmeister. Jealousy is his motive. His wife is smokin' hot, and finding out she was carrying on with the mayor of Crescent Cove of all people, a man nearly a decade his senior, had to have been quite the blow to his manly pride and ego. He carries a gun for protection 'cause he's kind of important, I guess. People like to feel they can defend themselves if the situation calls for it, so there's your method, and," she stressed, "he was there at the party, on the lawn at the time of the murder, as a matter of fact. Opportunity. Bam. You're welcome."

Desmond regarded her quietly for a moment. She could tell he was weighing her words very carefully as he sipped his coffee. Just when she was starting to grow impatient, he said, "All fine points, Ms. Holiday. With facts like that, it would be hard to deny he is the killer."

Juniper beamed.

"But I don't think he is."

Her jaw hit the floor. "Why?" she squawked, flailing her arms.

The hint of a smile touched his mouth. "Call it a gut feeling, Ms. Holiday."

Juniper spluttered. "You can't deny those are solid facts, Des. If I brought that to anyone else, they'd be on this guy like flies on stink."

"Anyone else is not me," Desmond said. "While I appreciate your insight, I can't just go off arresting folks without doing my due diligence. You know, checking things like if the caliber of a gun a suspect owns is the same caliber that shot the mayor and a suspect's supposed alibi and so on."

"Yeah, yeah, but you have to admit, Preston is a good suspect, and there aren't a lot of people on the list."

"Indeed. Maybe not on your list. But my list may be totally different," Mallard said, putting his cup down. He stood. "Thank you for the luncheon, Ms. Holiday. It was fantastic. I'll see myself out."

Juniper was too stunned to argue. So she sat there for a long minute after he'd vacated the premises, then she flopped back against the cushions and crossed her arms. "Son of a—"

CHAPTER NINETEEN

"Mallard sounded like he has some other suspects. I mean other than Preston," Juniper told Tori. "And he mentioned checking alibis and seeing what sorts of guns the suspects have. Do you have any idea how to find out what caliber bullet the mayor was shot with?"

Tori looked up from the computer. Her eyes were slightly unfocused. Beside her on the floor, curled up in his plush dog bed underneath a pile of covers, Barclay raised his head, his expression sleepy and annoyed.

"Hmm?" Tori said. "Yeah, that sounds like the sort of work the police do."

She went back to writing, and Barclay resituated himself, but then she looked up again, suddenly laser focused on Juniper, and Barclay perked up as well. "Was there a question in there?"

Juniper's sigh said without words how frustrated she was becoming with trying to pull Tori's attention from the story she was working on long enough to help her with her problem. "Yes, the bullet that shot Mayor Berkshaw. I need to find out what caliber it was, and then we can figure out who had that type of gun."

"It was small caliber, a single-shot type of gun."

Juniper gave her a look. "How in the world would you know?"

"Ah, which century are you living in again?" Tori pushed up the blue-blocker glasses she was wearing until they perched on top of her head. "It's all over the news, Juniper. You should watch sometime—or at least listen."

"Oh, hush up. I've been busy with other things. Haven't had time for television, and my music is all ad free. Commercial free. 'Cause it's all burned from my personal CD collection. Did they find the weapon?"

Tori gave her a look. If Juniper didn't know any better, she'd say Barclay gave her the same one but in dog form. "Again, maybe if you watched the news or listened to the radio, you would know they've not yet located a weapon, June."

"Humph. Well, I guess they haven't, or they'd have arrested someone, right?" Juniper headed for the door. "Thanks, Tor. You've helped a lot. I just need to figure out my next move."

"How about leaving it alone and letting the detectives do their job? That would be a good move, in my opinion!" Tori called after her, Barclay agreeing with a quiet "woof" before burying himself in his covers once again, eager to get back to his slumber.

Of course, Juniper ignored her. Might as well, she decided, because as soon as she left the room, she knew Tori would fall right back into her writing trance, where nothing existed but computer keys and the movie playing out in her head. "Don't wait supper for me. I might be out a while!"

Hopefully, she could find some answers down at Rotgut & Ruin, Juniper thought as she backed her car out of the garage. She needed some solid proof, something to take to Mallard. Mallard had given off the distinct vibe that he didn't think Preston was the killer or that he wasn't the only suspect. But who else could there be?

Chalis was in the clear, Madison Lane was in the clear, Susan Berkshaw had been at the airport… or had she? Mallard had mentioned checking alibis. But then there was William Walcroft. Junie's Spidey-sense told her there was something strange about that situation. His wife had said that he was trying to get a project going, but there was no proposal, according to Wanda.

And of course, there was the matchbook. Juniper knew that had to be a clue. And finally, who belonged to the coat that was left in her coat closet?

Hopefully, she would find some answers at Rotgut & Ruin. Even if the goblins knew nothing about the current mess in Crescent Cove, Theo made a mean strawberry daiquiri— the best in the Cove, to be honest. Those things were so smooth, Juniper had never once tasted the alcohol, and over the course of the past several years, she'd had quite a few of them to base her opinion on.

139

Rotgut & Ruin was nestled between two vacant stores in the seedier part of Crescent Cove. The place was about as popular with the locals as the steakhouse, RarelyDone, when it came to its food, even if all they offered was simply bar fare. There was something about it that kept 'em coming back for more.

Not everyone in the Cove knew this, but the bar was run by goblins, and goblins, as it turned out, were fantastic at making bar food. The only thing they did better was alcohol, which made sense. They were in the business of drink, after all.

Juniper and Theodosius, the owner, went

way back, actually. Only back then, she hadn't known Theo was a goblin. She'd stumbled onto that knowledge much as she had the rest of the paranormal folk of the Cove—accidentally. Funnily enough, it had been a full moon then, as well. She'd caught Theo exiting the bar through the back way where they got their deliveries, but he was decidedly greener than she'd ever seen him, and his ears were pointy, though that was a trait he kept even in his human disguise. People these days were altering different parts of themselves all the time, so it didn't raise too many brows, even in the Cove.

Naturally, she'd been sworn to secrecy and bound by a blood oath per the goblins' ways. They'd been friends before, and they remained friends now. And while the wolves kept an ear out for things she wouldn't be privy to otherwise, the goblins let her in on deals the world over. If she wanted a certain luxury item, they could usually point her in its direction without a fuss. It was how she got her hands on the antique piano in the music room. It was one of the first ever in circulation, and she would never have known about it if it weren't for Theo and his buddies.

But that wasn't what she was here for today. She was here for a drink and conversation, which she *hoped* would lead her somewhere interesting.

Juniper stepped inside the cozy atmosphere of the building. She immediately went to the bar and ordered a strawberry daiquiri.

"Is Theo not in today?" she asked the barkeep, Angelica, a stout lady a little taller than Juniper with biceps as big as Tori's head, long blond hair kept in a tight braid down her back, and the perfect face of makeup on her angular features.

"He had to step out for a sec," said Angelica, her sweet voice a direct contrast to her outward appearance. She sounded like a cartoony kid instead of a full-grown adult. "One of the trucks came in late, and he's unloading it now."

"Gotcha," Juniper said, nodding. Angelica set her daiquiri in front of her, and Juniper took a drink. It wasn't as smooth as Theo's, but it was darn close. "Angelica, don't let me have more than five of these suckers, m'kay?"

Angelica chuckled. "Sure thing, June, darlin'."

Juniper sat there, drinking her chilled alcoholic beverage and bobbing her head along to the music playing, drumming out the beat on her thighs with her hands while she waited for Theo to come back.

She was three daiquiris in by the time her goblin buddy walked back behind the bar.

"Nip-nop!" he greeted, which was his nickname for her, and he was the only one allowed to call her that. "I haven't seen you in ages! How've you been, lady mine?"

Juniper batted her lashes. "Stop, Theo, you're making me blush," she said, her words slightly slurred.

Theo laughed and started wiping down glasses. "How many of those have you had, Nippers?"

"Three," Angelica answered for her. "She's cut off after five."

Theo raised his brows at Juniper and shook his head, a smile on his face. "You know you're toast after two."

"I believe," she said, drawing out the word, "the word you're looking for is *buzzed*, buddy. And I am. Pleasantly so."

"All right," Theo said, sharing a look with

Angelica that Juniper should have been paying attention to, but she was having too much fun slurping the remainder of her drink from the bottom of her glass to pay attention to them or anyone else. "I'll handle the other two drinks, then."

"Niiice," Juniper said, grinning widely and drawing out the "*i*".

"So, did you just decide to get lit tonight, or did you secretly come to see me?" Theo teased as he made her fourth drink *without* alcohol, though she wouldn't notice.

"I just came by to boot the sheeze, Theo, baby."

"That so?" He plunked the glass in front of her, and she immediately wrapped her lips around the straw and took a long drink.

"Yup." She burped. Loudly. And then proceeded to spill every bit of information about the Berkshaw case she knew, ending with, "It's a real shame nobody else knows anything, Theo. Real shame."

"Well, now, I might be able to help you out, Nippers, but you gotta sober up first. Otherwise you won't remember a thing."

Before Juniper could defend her sobriety, he

put a glass of something murky in front of her and told her to hold her nose and drink it in one go. Grimacing, Juniper did so, and she nearly had a coughing fit after the vile potion was swallowed.

"Good grief, Theo," she complained. "That stuff is horrid."

"It works, though."

She couldn't deny that. She was as sober as a nun now. Smacking her lips at the aftertaste, she propped her arms on the bar and said, "Tell me what you know."

"I hear a lot here at the bar. For example, there were some extramarital activities going on at the Berkshaw house."

Juniper snapped her fingers. "I knew it! So Preston Lane *did* have a motive!"

"Preston? Why would he have a motive?"

Juniper was confused. "Madison Lane was the one the mayor was having the affair with. He must have found out. I bet he was very angry."

"The mayor? He wasn't the one having the affair. It was his wife."

"What?" Juniper almost fell off her chair.

"But she told me she thought her husband was having one."

Theo shrugged. "Probably trying to throw you off track. Who would have an affair with *him*? I don't think he was having one. I would have heard. I'm privy to almost every rumor in town. But I know for a fact that Susan was."

"How do you know that?"

"She was sitting at this very bar, and I over-heard her on the phone. She was whispering, but I have big ears." Theo pointed to his ears. "A lot of people don't realize how good my hearing is. Anyway, she was saying something about how Floyd would never find out, and they could be together soon as long as the other person got a divorce."

"Who was she talking to?" Juniper asked, even though she already had an idea.

Theo threw the towel he'd been using to clean glasses over his shoulder. "I couldn't tell you that."

It was all starting to click for Juniper now. She had one last question to find an answer to. "You wouldn't happen to know who wears a fur coat with a mink face on the collar, would you? Someone left it at my party."

"That's not really the type of coat my clientele wears." Theo gestured around the bar.

Good point. Rotgut & Ruin was strictly a jeans-and-leather type of bar.

"What you need is to find some pictures of fancy events. You should check out Gina Dodd's blog. She puts all the pictures she takes that don't make it into articles there."

She thanked Theo for his information and Angelica for the drinks then sped home, eager to tell Tori about her new suspicions… and then figure out what she was going to do about them.

CHAPTER TWENTY-ONE

"June?" Tori called from the doorway to Juniper's office.

She raised her head from staring at the computer screen and focused on her goddaughter. "Hmm? What's up, Tori-bori?"

"Nothing really. Just wanted to apologize for being short with you earlier. I was knee-deep into a very enthralling scene, and when I get distracted, my train of thought derails…"

Juniper shooed Loki out from in front of the computer screen and gave Tori an odd look. "No, I think you were as tall then as you are now, dear."

"Oh, good grief." Tori snorted then

laughed. "Very funny, Juniper. Anyway, I thought I should say sorry. I wasn't trying to be rude. Was just trying to write while the muse was whispering into my ear."

"I hope your muse was male and it was tons of sweet nothings he whispered." Juniper waggled her eyebrows, a slight smile curving her lips. "It's all good, Tori. I'm fine, you're fine. We can move on now."

"All right." Tori moved away from the doorframe and walked into the room. She picked up and cuddled Finn, who had been lying behind the monitor, before walking over to stand behind Juniper and look over her shoulder. "What are you looking at? Pictures? What are these?"

Juniper clicked on one of the pictures. It showed the entrance of the movie theater downtown with cars lined up and people making their way inside in gowns and fancy attire. "This is Gina Dodd's blog. Who knew the woman took so many pictures? This one is the fancy movie screening they had last year. Recognize that coat?"

Tori squinted and looked closer at the screen then glanced at the guest chair, where Juniper had draped the coat that had been left in the closet. "That's the one that was left here. Who is that wearing it?"

Juniper enlarged the photo. "Susan Berkshaw."

"Oh… I guess that makes sense then. She was probably so upset she left without it."

Juniper shook her head. "Nope. I distinctly remember she was wearing a white fur. There was a little bit of blood on it from when she knelt down beside her husband, and I remember thinking about the stark contrast of red on white."

Tori put Finn down and looked at Juni. "But why would she have two coats here? Maybe she let someone borrow the other one."

"I have a theory. It explains everything. Theodosius at the gob… err Rotgut & Ruin said that it was Susan who was having an affair, not the mayor."

"*That* I can believe. The mayor wasn't exactly passionate affair material."

"You can say that again." Juniper shuddered at the thought of having an affair with the mayor. "Anyway, Theo overheard a phone conversation she was having where she told the other person that the mayor had no idea and they could be together soon."

"Wait, didn't Susan tell you that she suspected her husband of having an affair?"

"Yes, but I think that was just a distraction to muddy the waters and keep the police from looking at *her*."

"So you think whoever she was having an affair with killed the mayor?" Tori said.

"Actually, I think Susan killed him."

"But Susan wasn't here. She RSVP'd that she'd be out of town and only showed up *after* he was shot."

Ludo had hopped back onto the desk and was parading in front of the monitor. Juniper pushed his tail out of her face. "That's what she wanted everyone to think, but what if she was actually at the party the whole time?" Juniper remembered how Mallard had stressed checking alibis. Perhaps he'd found some discrepancy in Susan's.

Tori gave her a look as if Juniper's theory was far-fetched. "Wouldn't someone have noticed her? I mean, I know we all had masks, but it wasn't *that* hard to figure out who was who."

"Remember that mysterious woman in the silver gown? She skulked around in the shadows, and I never really saw her talking to anyone. In fact, she avoided people."

"You think that was Susan?" Tori tilted her head as she contemplated that. "How does the coat play in?"

"What if she came intending to shoot her husband? She wore the mink to the party and hid the gun in the pocket. No one was checking pockets when people arrived, just after the shooting."

"Okay, then what?"

"She skulks around, waiting for everyone to be outside when the fireworks go off. It's the perfect time to shoot the mayor because everyone was looking at the sky. Maybe she hoped no one would hear the gunshot and it would give her time to get away. I thought it was just noise from the fireworks, myself."

"True. Not too many noticed he'd even been shot for quite some time."

Juniper nodded. "So she shoots him and drops the gun into the ice bucket then rejoins the party like nothing happened."

"Hmm. Maybe. But if she rejoined the

party, then how did she come running from the driveway? That was only about five or ten minutes after he'd been shot, and she wasn't wearing a gown."

"Good point." Juniper petted Ludo as she contemplated that. "She must have shot him then run off. She could have run to her car and changed then rushed in, pretending she heard about it on the car radio. She probably knew Gina would get it out on the airwaves immediately."

"I suppose that could have happened."

"What if she dropped the gun in the ice bucket after she shot him then slipped it into the pocket of the white fur when she arrived? It was a small caliber and would fit in a pocket. The police didn't search her, just the other guests, and that would explain why they never found it on a guest or the premises."

Tori stood back, hands on hips. "You should call Detective Mallard."

"The detective didn't accept my theories before nor did he accept any of the evidence from the ghosts. Ol' Duckbutt is such a stickler for physical evidence, I'm afraid I can't speak to him about this until I have something solid."

Laughter sputtered from Tori's lips. "Well, June, you know how Desmond can be when it comes to things like courtrooms and facts and witnesses people can actually see."

"Oh, so it's *Desmond* now, is it? Yech. Y'all young people gross me out, using actual first names instead of high formality and all that," Juniper teased.

Tori looked worried now. "June, this is serious. I think you should let him handle it."

"Don't worry. I'll call him. Just as soon as I get some solid proof." Juniper picked up the mink coat from the chair and headed out the door.

CHAPTER TWENTY-TWO

Thirty minutes later, Juniper pulled up in front of the Berkshaw residence. It was a large, elegant home with a brick facade and perfectly trimmed shrubs.

She went up to the door and knocked. A moment later, Susan answered the door. A look of surprise came over her face when she saw Juniper standing there.

"Juniper," she said. "What a surprise. What brings you by?"

Juniper thrust the coat out. "I think this is your coat, isn't it?"

"Oh my, yes, it is. I must have forgotten it the other night with the tragedy." Susan managed to produce a few tears. "Won't you come in?"

Juniper followed Susan into an all-white living room. White couch, white rug, white brick fireplace. The woman loved white.

"Coffee?" Susan asked.

"No thanks. I won't be here that long. I was just wondering why you needed to wear two coats to my New Year's Eve party."

Susan managed to look taken aback. "I'm sure I don't know what you are talking about. I wasn't at your party. I came after... after..." Susan managed to produce more tears.

"Really? Oh, funny. I thought I saw you in a silver gown, lurking around. I know William Walcroft was looking for you. Did you know he asked his wife for a divorce?"

Susan's mask slipped for a second, and she stiffened but recovered quickly. "I don't know what that has to do with anything."

"I think you can stop lying now. The police have looked into your flight schedule, and it turns out you weren't exactly at the airport when your husband was shot." Juniper was lying, but she was pretty sure that was the case.

Mallard had given her the clue whether he realized it or not.

Susan's eyes narrowed. "If anyone shot my husband, it was that Madison Lane or maybe her husband."

"Nice try. I think it was you… or maybe William Walcroft. His wife saw him sneaking in to visit you right here at the mansion. It's only a matter of time before that gets out around the Cove." Donna had thought William was visiting the mayor for his secret project, but since there really was no project, Juniper assumed that he'd been here to see Susan. Maybe Donna had seen him, and he'd had to lie about it. This little tidbit seemed to be the tipping point for Susan.

"Fine. You think you're so smart. But you're not. In fact, it was dumb of you to come here. Because I'm not going to let you ruin things for me now that I've come this far!" Susan moved to the doorway, blocking Juniper's exit.

"What I don't understand is why you dressed up for the party. You could have just snuck around the side and shot him." Juniper wasn't about to leave without a full confession.

"You really are dumb. I had to come because I needed to wait for Floyd to be in just the right position where he was away from everyone else. I didn't want to shoot someone by mistake. Lucky for me, it was during the fireworks, which helped mask the sound."

"And then you put the gun in the giant ice bucket. Why not just take it to your car?"

"How do you think it would look if someone caught me running down the driveway in my gown with a gun?" Susan said. "I was planning to say I was running from the shooter if I did get caught, but as it turned out, no one even saw me."

"And then when you came back to play the grieving widow, you pocketed the gun, knowing no one would search you."

"Correct!" Susan looked very pleased with herself. "I tried to get the coat I'd worn to the party out of the closet, but I didn't get a second to myself, unfortunately."

"Did you dispose of the gun?" Juniper asked.

Susan's smile turned devious. "No. I figured I would never be a suspect. Which I wouldn't be if it wasn't for you. So… looks like the gun will come in handy again." Susan opened the drawer of a small table, pulled out the gun, and aimed it at Juniper.

Juniper put her hands up in front of her. Darn, she hadn't anticipated this! "Hold on there. You can't shoot me here. It will ruin all your white rugs and furniture."

"I don't plan to shoot you here. Out back." She gestured with the gun.

Juniper shuffled along in front of her, trying to think of how she could talk her way out of this. Maybe she'd be able to overpower her somehow.

"It's a shame you were so distraught over my husband's death that you came here to do yourself in," Susan said.

Juniper laughed. "I don't think anyone is going to believe that."

"Probably not." Susan shoved her in the back with the barrel of the gun. "Open the kitchen door and step out back."

Juniper did as told, looking around for a weapon she could use.

"No, it makes more sense that you were so upset that Floyd didn't respond to your advances that *you* were the one who killed him at your party.

Yes, it makes sense now. And then you came here to kill me since you were jealous that he picked me over you." Susan's laugh sounded a tad maniacal.

Juniper turned around to face her. They were standing in an open area with not even a stick to use as a weapon. Juni would have to just lunge toward the crazy woman and hope to wrestle the gun away.

"But when you tried to kill me with the same gun you shot Floyd with… the gun you stole from my house… we wrestled, and you ended up getting shot instead." Susan raised the gun.

"You got that wrestle over the gun part right." Juniper lunged to the right, but Susan was good with her aim. She jumped back and cocked the gun. Just before she fired, Juniper saw a ghostly figure go right through her.

Wait… was that Lionel?

Susan shuddered, and the shot went in the direction of the woods, giving Juniper the opportunity to jump on her and push her to the ground. She grabbed the gun and sat on Susan.

"Lionel, are you here?" She looked around for his ghostly figure but saw nothing. Had that been her imagination? She hadn't realized that the ghosts could even leave the vicinity of her mansion.

"The shot came from over here!" she heard someone yell.

Detective Mallard, Ackers, and Nichols came running around the corner of the house, stopping dead in their tracks when they saw Juniper and Susan.

"Well, well, well. If it isn't Duckman to the rescue," Juniper said, even though she didn't want to admit she was happy to see them.

CHAPTER TWENTY-THREE

"You should have left things to the police, but thanks for recording the confession," Desmond said as Juniper handed him the miniature tape recorder she'd had hidden in her purse.

"You're welcome." Juniper turned to watch Ackers place Susan Berkshaw in the back of his police car after having read her her rights. "Well, there's that one in the bag, Detective. Here's hoping it'll be our last."

Desmond shot her a look. "I hoped as much for the last three, Ms. Holiday. At this point, it's probably time to go with a little more than that."

"Such as? What can possibly be stronger than hope, Detective?"

"A restraining order?" came the response neither was expecting... and it was from the chief of police himself. "You are hereby ordered to leave this premises, Ms. Holiday. Detective Mallard, once you are done here, I expect to see you in my office."

"Yes, sir." Desmond nodded. "I'm almost done now. I'll meet you at the precinct in fifteen minutes."

Once he was gone, Juniper tapped Desmond on the shoulder to get his attention. "Are you in hot water, Duckster?"

"Most likely, Ms. Holiday, but don't worry yourself over it." He squared his shoulders. "I can handle myself."

Juniper's brows rose. "Yes, but can you handle the chief of police? He looks like a brutish sort of man."

"All bark and no bother," Desmond told her, his voice lower than it had been. "Go home, Juniper. Get a good night's sleep. Let your mind rest."

"I'll need it," she told him. "Because I've only a few weeks left to get everything in order for my Valentine's Day Card and Gift Exchange and Raffle."

"Already thinking about the next party." Desmond shook his head. "Is there anything you won't celebrate, Ms. Holiday?"

"I'll have to think about it, Detective," Juniper told him as she ducked into her car. "It's doubtful, though. There's not much I can think of that's not worth celebrating." Her grin lit her face and her eyes. She closed her car door, started the engine, and put the vehicle in drive. "See you soon, Duckman!"

As she drove away, thunderous music filled the air behind her, leaving the detective and his men shaking their heads in amused awe and confusion, because when it came to figuring out what drove Juniper Holiday, not one of them could find an answer.

"*L*ion-o… Yoo-hoo… where are you? Come out, come out," Juniper yelled as soon as she walked in the door. No one else was around, which was good since Juniper wanted their conversation to be private.

She hung her coat on the antique oak coat-tree beside the door and made her way to her office. She leaned back in her chair and put her feet up on the desk then pulled a bag of pretzels out of her drawer and bit in. It turned out being held at gunpoint made one hungry.

"Lionel, buddy. You around?"

Lionel floated up through the floor. "Yes, mum. What do you need?"

Juniper felt relieved. She was sure it was her ghost butler that had intervened with Susan Berkshaw and was afraid that it had somehow harmed him. She gave him the once-over. He appeared to be fine.

Juniper put her feet down and sat up straight in her chair. "Give it to me straight. Was that you over at Susan Berkshaw's?"

Lionel's ghostly form turned slightly pink. Was he embarrassed? "Yes, mum. I sensed you might need some help."

Juniper replayed the scene in her mind. Susan had the gun pointed straight at her when she pulled the trigger. It was likely only by Lionel intervening and causing Susan to move that the bullet missed. "I think you might have saved my butt!"

"Any good butler would do that, ma'am." Lionel said modestly.

"And you are a very good butler," Juniper said.

Lionel puffed with pride. "Thank you."

"I wasn't aware you could leave the mansion grounds," Juniper said.

"It's not advised, mum, but I took the risk, as I sensed you were in trouble."

Juniper felt a rush of affection for the ghost. "That was brave, and I appreciate it. I do sincerely want to apologize for hurting your feelings about not being able to relay my instructions. I promise to keep you in the loop from now on."

"Very good, mum." Lionel smiled.

"So, are we good?" Juniper asked.

"We're more than good." Lionel bowed. "Now, if you don't need anything else, I must go check on Jacobi. He was quite upset at something Sabrina is cooking up in the kitchen."

"Please go. We don't want him to get upset."

Lionel floated through the bookcase, and Juniper leaned back in her chair, happy that things at the Holiday mansion were back to normal. Now that she knew the cause of the mayor's death had nothing to do with her, she felt a renewed vigor in celebrating every holiday with her famous parties. She popped open a can of soda, taking a few minutes to rest before she dug in to the plans for the next party. This one, for Valentine's, was going to be the best party yet!

****

Will Juniper's Valentine's party be ruined by a murder? Find out in My Fatal Valentine, the next book in the Juniper Holiday series!

Check out all Leighann Dobbs books at http://www.leighanndobbsbooks.com

3 Bodies and a Biscotti
Brownies, Bodies & Bad Guys
Bake, Battle & Roll
Wedded Blintz
Scones, Skulls & Scams
Ice Cream Murder
Mummified Meringues
Brutal Brulee (Novella)
No Scone Unturned
Cream Puff Killer
Never Say Pie

Lady Katherine Regency Mysteries
***

An Invitation to Murder (Book 1)
The Baffling Burglaries of Bath (Book 2)
Murder at the Ice Ball (Book 3)
A Murderous Affair (Book 4)
Murder on Charles Street (Book 5)

Hazel Martin Historical Mystery Series
***

Murder at Lowry House (book 1)
Murder by Misunderstanding (book 2)

Sam Mason Mysteries
(As L. A. Dobbs)

***

Telling Lies (Book 1)
Keeping Secrets (Book 2)
Exposing Truths (Book 3)
Betraying Trust (Book 4)
Killing Dreams (Book 5)

Romantic Comedy

***

Corporate Chaos Series

In Over Her Head (book 1)
Can't Stand the Heat (book 2)
What Goes Around Comes Around (book 3)
Careful What You Wish For (4)

Contemporary Romance

***

Reluctant Romance

Sweet Romance (Written As Annie Dobbs)

Firefly Inn Series

***

Another Chance (Book 1)

Another Wish (Book 2)

Hometown Hearts Series

***

No Getting Over You (Book 1)

A Change of Heart (Book 2)

Sweet Mountain Billionaires

***

Jaded Billionaire (Book 1)

A Billion Reasons Not To Fall In Love (Book 2)

————

Regency Romance

***

Scandals and Spies Series:

ABOUT THE AUTHOR

USA Today best-selling Author, Leighann Dobbs, has had a passion for reading since she was old enough to hold a book, but she didn't put pen to paper until much later in life. After a twenty-year career as a software engineer, with a few side trips into selling antiques and making jewelry, she realized you can't make a living reading books, so she tried her hand at writing them and discovered she had a passion for that, too! She lives in New Hampshire with her husband, Bruce, their trusty Chihuahua mix, Mojo, and beautiful rescue cat, Kitty.

Find out about her latest books by signing up at:
https://leighanndobbscozymysteries.gr8.com

Connect with Leighann on Facebook:
https://www.facebook.com/groups/718049055015420

This is a work of fiction.

None of it is real. All names, places, and events are products of the author's imagination. Any resemblance to real names, places, or events are purely coincidental, and should not be construed as being real.

Masquerade Party Murder

Copyright © 2022

Leighann Dobbs Publishing

http://www.leighanndobbs.com

All Rights Reserved.

No part of this work may be used or reproduced in any manner, except as allowable under "fair use," without the express written permission of the author.

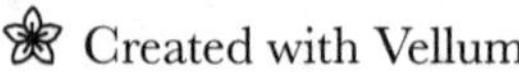 Created with Vellum